CONSEQUENCES

HEATHER DAWN GRAY

ISBN:978-1-9991-2024-5

DEDICATION

To those with the patience and understanding to stand by
my side and support me, even when I doubt myself…

especially you, Ron.

Other Novels By
HEATHER DAWN GRAY

THE LIE

WHERE TRUTH LIES

Available globally on Amazon

ACKNOWLEDGMENTS

Even during a pandemic, a book should not be created in isolation.

Special thanks to the following Beta Readers for making this novel a better version of itself: Rod Baker, Christine Berstad, Debbie Bhangoo, Lenore Delday, Nick Forster, Delia Gray, Frank Kitching, Mike Marshall, Elizabeth Richards, Colby Starman, Ron Starman, and Melody Stewart. Your keen attention to detail, specialized areas of expertise, and kind dedication to helping me, made it that much better.

Also, a very special thank you to Stephen Ewashko for once again finessing my ideas and creating an amazing cover.

CHAPTER ONE
January 17, 2018

The Cessna descended from the murky sky and skidded to a stop in the wet, sparsely seeded field. If it hadn't been for a driver in a car parked close by, no one would have witnessed its arrival.

Eventually a passenger emerged from a rectangle of light cast by the open door, and made his way down the metal stairs. He stepped onto the field, and glanced down, mud squelching over the toe of his Bordeaux leather Gucci's. An exhausted sigh escaped into the night. Juggling his luggage, he crept out of the way as the plane's stairs retracted, and it taxied to the end of the field before disappearing into the fog of low hanging clouds.

The nearby Lincoln Town car roared to life, and the shadow hobbled toward it, climbing into the back seat. He rubbed his shoes on the carpet, the corners of his mouth turned down in disgust. A container of wet wipes appeared from the front seat, and he grabbed it without a word.

Soon the street lights and random headlights flickered inside the car. The chauffeur scrutinized him in the rear-view mirror. The man glared back. The driver cleared his throat and returned his attention to the road as the wipers tapped out a monotonous cadence. Eventually the car stopped in front of the Delta Hotel where the man climbed out, taking his briefcase and suitcase with him. The mud and wet ones remained in the car as it drove away.

Once in his suite, he flicked on the TV and closed the curtains. His watch informed him it was ten fifty-five. He pulled out his phone and sent a text.

Boots on the ground.

The hour's news loop would begin with the top stories at eleven. He surveyed the stocked bar and removed a cognac sampler, pouring it into a crystal glass from the cupboard. Loosening his tie, and un-tucking his shirt, he leaned back on the leather sofa, placing his feet on the black moulded coffee table. The amber liquid slid down his throat, and he closed his eyes.

"After twenty-four years, the police have detained a suspect for the 1994 murder of Lori Trembley."

His eyes snapped open. He leaned forward and placed his glass on the table where his feet once rested. A photo of the suspect filled the screen. The man's chest tightened. There was no mistaking the identity of the man staring back at him.

"Police say evidence led them to a former Clark Park Gang member still living on Vancouver's East side. The sixty-year-old suspect's lawyer, April Somersby, gave this statement following the bail hearing today."

He leaned closer to the TV, studying April. Her voice belied her petite stature; booming, authoritative, a person to be reckoned with.

"My client, is innocent. He has a good reputation in the community. Please suspend judgement until we have our day in court. Remember, citizens are innocent until proven guilty."

The man emptied his glass and let the liquid heat soothe his nerves. At least the lawyer appeared to be adequate. He flicked off the TV, and for the first time, surveyed the hotel suite. The penthouse windows overlooked the harbour, twinkling lights visible in the distance. He hung the robe from the bedroom closet on the back of the bathroom door, turned on the shower, and slipped out of his clothes. He carefully hung his Armani suit beside the robe, noticing traces of mud on the hem of the pants. He'd have to get them sent for dry cleaning in the morning. Not that he'd be wearing that suit anytime soon. *Damn hicksville town.* The steaming water soothed his taut muscles. He watched the drops slide off his freshly waxed chest, down his long thighs, the soap pooling around his feet. It had been many years since he'd graced the streets of Vancouver. He swore he'd never return. But here he was.

The coconut aroma of the body wash transported him to a better place. Somewhere he'd rather be, and he languished for a few minutes in the fantasy playing out behind closed eyes. Turquoise waters, palm trees and Latin music. *If only.*

His eyes snapped open, and he stepped out of the shower onto the plush mat and toweled off with a thick bath sheet before slipping into the soft white robe. He sauntered into the bar area and surveyed the inventory. A twelve-year Macallan caught his overtired gaze, and he reached for it, unscrewing the cap and pouring it into a new glass. Perhaps it would take the edge off and lead him into a deep sleep.

The silence didn't comfort him, but rather grated on his nerves. He swigged the Scotch back and let the robe drop to the floor. His naked body slid between thousand count percale sheets, under a feather duvet. Still, sleep eluded him. Behind eyelids heavy with the burdens of a botched job years ago, and now this unanticipated connection, his mind replayed events he'd spent a lifetime trying to forget.

CHAPTER TWO
January 13, 2018 (Four Days Earlier)

"Message from fleet headquarters. No enemy vessels in the area. Proceed." The submarine bridge speaker crackled to life and the Russian officer paced, contradicting his bravado and claims of familiarity with such a mission.

Paul held his breath as he withdrew into this unfamiliar world, turning the page to continue the voyage, when the doorbell rang, pulling him from the bottom of the ocean and back into his living room.

"Don't move a muscle. I'll get it." Nora strode in from the kitchen, swinging a tea towel over her shoulder and patting his foot hanging off the end of the couch on her way by.

The fog lifted. "Sorry honey." It was more of an unconscious mutter to himself than anyone else. He glanced at the rain streaking down the picture window. His mind returned to the bridge, but the creak of the front door didn't allow him to fully transition back into the underwater world.

I need to spray those hinges with WD40. But the sound stirred something more than maintenance worries within him, and he took a deep breath to quieten the anxiety rising in his throat. It'd been a long time, and yet an unexpected door bell sent him back to where he swore, he'd never return.

The words on the page lost their meaning. He laid the book on his chest and listened for the voices he expected to hear; a kid in the community soliciting money for soccer or swimming or God knows what. Young families bought into the neighbourhood again after it aged up. It was nice to hear children laughing. While the solicitations were getting out of hand, it would have been comforting to hear their voices at his door rather than the deep voice resonating down the hall.

"Good afternoon, Ma'am, is Paul Giovanni home?"

Paul's heart quickened.

"Honey?" Nora's tone, half an octave higher than usual, yet steady and in control, followed.

After twenty-two years of marriage, he recognized the lilt to her voice as her 'there's trouble tone'. She used the voice when she needed a spider killed, or thought they'd stayed at a party long enough and it was time to go home.

The book fell to the floor as he swung his legs over the side of the couch, sat up, and ran a hand through his hair in one fluid motion. He stepped over the book, and glanced out the living room window. A police cruiser sat next to the curb. His curb. He swallowed and forced himself to put one foot in front of the other. *There's no reason to fear the police at my door.*

Nora's face at the end of the hallway reflected her inner turmoil. His feet moved his body toward her and he placed a hand on her shoulder, shifting himself in front to shield her from whatever these officers had to say.

"Paul Giovanni?" The shorter officer peered up at Paul, straightening as he did so.

"Yes?" Paul knew better than to expand on the required answers to police questions. He racked his brain trying to figure out why two police officers stood on his step on a quiet Saturday afternoon in 2018. He should ask them in out of the rain, but the attitude emanating from the short cop deterred him from showing any type of hospitality.

The taller of the two stamped the water from his boots. "Mr. Giovanni, mind if we step inside?"

Paul exhaled and glanced past the police officers. Mrs. Campbell, sporting a 1970s era Adidas velour tracksuit, peered through her picture window across the street. *Great. The whole neighbourhood will hear about this.*

He took a step back. "Uh, yeah, okay." He opened the screen door, and he and Nora backed down the hallway, the door latching behind the two men. They took off their caps, a stream of water splashing to the floor beside them as they did so. Each man reached into his pocket to produce identification.

The shorter of the two pointed to himself, then to his partner. "I'm Detective West and this is Detective Berstad."

Paul stared at them, the pit of his stomach churning. What could they want? Then his mind turned to Zoe.

"Our daughter, Zoe, is she okay? Has something happened?" Paul felt his knees go weak, and he glanced back at Nora's ashen face. His heart thumped in his chest.

Detective Berstad raised his hand between them and shook his head. "Zoe's fine. This isn't about her. At least not directly." His expression remained neutral, dark eyes expressionless.

Paul tilted his head and glanced at Nora, who raised her eyebrows, then cleared her throat. "Do you want to come in? Is this going to take long?" Nora backed down the hallway and motioned to the living room.

Paul stood his ground. They weren't getting into his home until he knew what this was about.

Detective West glanced down at his wet boots. "No, no, that's fine. I hope this won't take long. Let's just get to it, shall we?"

Paul crossed his arms and waited, trying to appear relaxed, but the muscles in his jaw divulged the grind of his teeth. Nora returned to his side and rested her arm on his back.

Berstad cleared his throat and stared into Paul's eyes. "We have a couple of questions for you before we proceed."

Paul inhaled, meeting the detective's stare but remained silent.

"Are you the biological father of Zoe Giovanni, who currently lives in Edmonton and attends the University of Alberta?"

Paul furrowed his brows and turned his head. "Yes, but you said Zoe's okay. What's going on?"

"Yes, yes, Zoe's fine. We're investigating a cold case. Zoe became known to us and led us to you." Detective Berstad held up his hand to stop Paul from protesting. "It's complicated, but Zoe posted DNA results to GENmatch. It seems her DNA matches to the suspect in our case as a daughter. This led us to you."

Paul stiffened. "Is this some kind of joke?"

"No, it's no joke. We'd like to take you down to the station, Mr. Giovanni. You're our number one suspect in a cold case. From Zoe's results, it appears your DNA was found in blood at the scene of the murder of Lori Trembley on April 17, 1994. We need to question you at the station and have your blood tested for confirmation." He cleared his throat again, and his eyes met Paul's, unwavering.

Paul's arms dropped to his sides, and he backed up to the wall for support. His breath caught in his throat and his head swirled.

It was Nora's turn to step in front of him. "This is ridiculous. There must be a mistake."

"I'm afraid not... Mrs. Giovanni, I assume?" West stepped forward off the mat. A hint of a smile played at the corners of his mouth, like this was some kind of game.

Nora nodded, indicating she was indeed Mrs. Giovanni.

"We just need to ask some questions and get a blood test. At this stage, we're gathering information." He turned his attention to Paul. "Please get your coat, and come with us."

Paul inhaled before straightening and shuffling over to the hall closet. Best to cooperate. He slid his arms into his raincoat, then turned to Nora. He cradled her chin, staring into her eyes. Her gaze grounded him like it always did, and his mind cleared. "Call Jenna and ask for the contact details of the lawyer that represented her son when he was in trouble last year. Then call the lawyer and ask her to meet me at the station."

Nora nodded, a tear sliding down her cheek. Paul wrapped his arms around her, and in a husky voice whispered in her ear. "It's going to be alright. I had nothing to do with this. It's all a big misunderstanding."

Nora brought her hand up to her face and wiped away the tears. "I know, Paul. I know."

Paul glanced back as he descended the stairs to the front yard. Nora stood rooted to the spot. He called back over his shoulder. "Call Jenna, Nora."

Mrs. Campbell from across the street pushed open her door to get a better look, bringing the glasses hanging around her neck to the bridge of her nose.

Paul slid into the back of the cruiser, like he'd done so many years before.

April 17, 1994? He knew exactly where he was. His stomach dropped, and bile rose in the back of his throat. Twenty-four years later, Lori Trembley's ghost came back to haunt him.

CHAPTER THREE
January 13, 2018

Paul focused on the street in front of the police cruiser. He didn't want to revisit Mrs. Campbell gawking from her front step, or glimpse the fear on Nora's face before she turned away and phoned the lawyer.

He stared past the back of West's head, barely rising above the headrest. Suddenly, knuckles banged on the glass partition. Paul lurched forward, his hand slamming against the partition.

Berstad, in the driver's seat, stared at him in the rear-view mirror. "We'll stop at the hospital to get a blood sample."

His muffled words vibrated through the glass separating them. It wasn't a question, but the detective's eyes held the question mark missing in his voice.

Paul's eyes widened. "Do you have a warrant for that? Which hospital?"

West reached into his breast pocket pulling out a paper that he slowly unfolded and held against the partition in front of Paul. "Vancouver General. Why, where would you prefer?" Sarcasm laced West's question, even through the partition.

"I work at that hospital as an orderly, and Nora's the lab manager. Any chance you can pick another hospital?" Paul's heart raced. He'd given up his mechanic's job five years ago to become an orderly at the hospital. How would it look, him coming in flanked by police officers? Hell, he knew most of the staff.

"Too bad you don't get to choose…"

Berstad cut off his partner. "Sorry, but they have the testing facilities we need and they're expecting us to bring someone in today." The two men glanced at each other, but Paul could only see Berstad's face and it reflected a message for his partner to stand down.

The rest of the trip progressed in silence. Too quickly, the car slid into the emergency bay, and West opened his door. Paul stepped out of the car and entered the hospital, flanked by both detectives. Eyes gazed blankly from exhausted faces in the waiting room. If he had to wait like everyone else, it'd be hours. He stared at the floor, hoping no one recognized him. Berstad spoke to someone behind a plexiglass partition and then tilted his head toward a room around the corner. Paul, with West at his elbow, followed obediently into the room. Someone with a tray of needles and tubes stepped through the door shortly after. Paul breathed a sigh of relief. No one he recognized. The detective handed her a paper and labels he'd received from the plexiglass lady, and she asked Paul his name, birthdate and healthcare number. He reached into his pocket and pulled out his wallet, then his health card.

The phlebotomist studied the card, then Paul, then the card again.

"Is your wife Nora…"

"Excuse me, this is police business. Keep you questions to those required to do your job."

Paul glanced at Detective Berstad, grateful for the interjection. The needle glinted in the fluorescent lights before she embedded it in his arm.

The name tag fixed above the pocket on the lab coat in front of him read 'Jen'. He'd have to let Nora know Jen was asking inappropriate questions. *Poor Nora. What would happen at work on Monday?* The rumours would be rampant.

He stared at the tube of blood filling from his arm. Its mauve top visible through the plastic vacutainer holder. The same blood they said they found at the scene. His blood. But how could it be his blood? Their DNA test was wrong. Or maybe Zoe entered her DNA results incorrectly into the system. Paul breathed a sigh of relief, but the pit of his stomach burned. Zoe was meticulous. It wouldn't be like her to make a mistake with data entry.

He watched the phlebotomist and Detective West initial the papers and a piece of tape across the top of the tube of blood. His blood. They held his life in their hands.

Paul returned to the cruiser and Berstad maneuvered the car around two ambulances that arrived in their absence.

"Busy day. Seems there's nothing better to do on a rainy Saturday." West nodded toward another ambulance entering the bay. "Glad I never became a paramedic. I can't imagine sticking around hospitals all day long waiting for your patient to be admitted. Complete waste of time, in my humble opinion.

"System's broken for sure."

Paul leaned back against the pleather seat. The faint smell of vomit and body odour brought up memories of previous back seat rides he'd rather forget.

The car stopped, and he felt the gears shift into park. His eyes snapped open. He waited while the detectives chatted, then pulled open his door. He swung his legs out, then rose, slamming his head into the steel door frame.

"Shit!" He grabbed his head, catching the grin of Detective West. He glared through squinted eyes and continued. "Not something a little guy like you has to worry about."

The detective's grin turned to a scowl. He turned and walked into the station, holding the door momentarily before letting it swing back.

What am I doing? No sense making enemies I don't need right now. Paul caught the door with his foot and traipsed in, head down.

"Interrogation room two. She's waiting for you." A woman behind plexiglass pointed down the hall. *What had the world come to that everyone needed to be protected?* Paul caught himself. The police thought he committed murder; that's what the world had come to.

Berstad opened the door to the interrogation room. A slender, middle-aged woman sat at a table. She set her phone down and rose, extending a hand toward Paul.

"April Somersby. You must be Paul? Your wife called me. Didn't think I'd beat you to the station?" April glanced at the police officers standing in the doorway.

"We stopped at the hospital, where Paul gave us a blood sample."

April's head snapped to Paul and then back to West. "A blood sample? I hope you had a warrant for that?"

West pulled the piece of paper from his breast pocket. "Yes ma'am." He smiled triumphantly.

April grabbed the warrant and studied it. "Can I have a few minutes with my client before you ask questions?"

"Sure, we need a coffee anyway. Back in a few."

The door closed behind them and Paul slumped into a chair beside April.

"Okay, why were you brought in? Your wife said something about DNA linking you to a murder?"

Paul ran a hand through his hair and leaned back in his chair. "Yeah. It seems my daughter uploaded her DNA results to GENmatch. They match as a daughter to the DNA of blood found at the scene of a crime back in 1994. I don't have a clue what they're talking about." Paul leaned forward and studied April's eyes. "I swear to you I've murdered no one."

"Okay, we can talk about the details later. Let's find out what they want to ask. I'll interject if I don't think you should answer. And don't elaborate; just answer the questions, understand?"

"I do." Paul stared at the floor before raising his eyes to hers once more. "Thanks for being here."

The door swung open, and the detectives reappeared, coffees in hand. They slid into chairs across the table and set their steaming cups on the surface between them. Normally, the aroma of coffee would have Paul searching for the nearest coffee shop, but today it turned his stomach.

"Now tell us, Paul, where were you on the night of April 17, 1994?" West leaned forward.

Paul shrugged and paused before responding. "That was a long time ago."

West continued, unphased. "Do you recognize the name Lori Trembley?"

Paul grinned and raised his head to meet West's gaze. "Why yes I do."

West glanced at his partner, who leaned forward. "How's that? Why do you recognize that name?"

"You don't have to answer that." April put her arm across the table as if protecting Paul from a sudden stop.

Paul moved her arm away and leaned forward. "You mentioned it at the house when you brought me in for questioning." This wasn't Paul's first interrogation, and he almost enjoyed getting back in the saddle. If only the situation wasn't so serious.

"Gentlemen. I'm not sure what your rush is. You don't have DNA confirmation that Paul's even a viable suspect. Is this necessary right now?" April placed her hand on Paul's shoulder. "In fact, Paul, if you agree, I think it's best you don't answer any further questions."

Paul spread his arms, palms up. "Your call Ms. Somersby. If I don't have to answer questions right now, I'd prefer to be home on the couch, finishing the book I was reading when I was so rudely interrupted." Paul noted the disappointed expressions on the detectives' faces. They knew it was over, at least for today.

April drove Paul home. Mrs. Campbell, wine glass in one hand, cigarette in the other, peeked out of her picture window as they drove by. He'd made her day.

April Somersby pulled her sports car into the driveway, and Paul stared up at his house. He noted the paint peeling on the window trim. Why hadn't he noticed that before? The living room curtain moved and Nora peered out.

"Thanks for the lift... and everything." It seemed inadequate, but he didn't know what else to say. She'd peppered him with questions all the way home until he asked her to stop. He couldn't deal with it right now.

"Call me when you're ready to have an in-depth conversation." April reached into her blazer pocket and handed him a business card.

"I will. And thanks again." Paul stepped onto the wet pavement, closing the door behind him. April backed her car down the driveway, and he inhaled. The smell of fresh rain calmed him, and he closed his eyes before taking another deep breath.

The rattle of the screen door brought him back to reality. Nora stood in the doorway with blotchy cheeks and puffy eyes. He forced a smile and climbed the three stairs into her arms. Was she angry at him? She'd told him long ago she was done with his sordid past.

Nora grasped him tightly, sobbing into his chest. He clung to her, relief flooding his body and strengthening his resolve. He would prove his innocence. They held each other; the cool fresh breeze wafting through the doorway. At last, Paul looked up and cast a glance over his shoulder. Mrs. Campbell's hefty frame filled her front entrance. She was brazen enough to continue staring when he shot her a steely stare.

"Nora, let's go sit down and talk about this."

She relaxed her embrace and stepped back. "Why Paul? Why are they doing this?"

Paul closed the door, leaving Mrs. Campbell to speculate about why he left in a police cruiser and returned in a sporty Lexus. "I don't know. I truly don't." He rested his hand on her back and guided her to the living room.

"Before we get started, I'm going to make myself some tea. Do you want some?" It was Nora's attempt at normalcy. A cup of tea made her feel better.

He would have loved some whisky, but he'd given that up years ago. "No, I'm fine thanks."

Nora left the room and Paul picked up his novel from the floor, placing it on the side table. He sat on the couch and leaned forward, head in his hands, until the sound of Nora's cup settling on the oak coffee table knocked him out of his stupor. He shook his head and leaned back. Nora perched on the couch beside him. He instinctively patted her knee.

"I'm so sorry, Nora. Years ago, I promised you the police would have no reason to knock on our door. This is a complete surprise to me. I didn't see it coming."

"I know, I know." Her words rang hollow. Like she knew she had to say them, but didn't mean them. How could she? She didn't know.

Hell, he didn't know.

"So, what kinds of questions did they ask you?"

Paul hesitated. *What had they asked?* "Not much. April stopped the interview saying they didn't even have my blood test results, so there was no reason for them to question me yet. They weren't happy about having to let me go." Paul turned to her and held her gaze. "But they took me to the General where I had my blood taken. I'm so sorry, honey. The phlebotomist was Jen. She recognized my name and asked me if I was your husband. This won't make things easy for you at work."

Nora's face flushed. She lifted the cup to her lips, and took a sip before responding. "She knows better than to ask questions like that. No one will dare speak to me about the rumours. Patient confidentiality rules and all. Why'd they have to take you to the General?"

"I asked to go somewhere else, but they said the General had the testing facilities they needed." Paul ran a hand through his hair and noticed his knee bouncing up and down. He stilled it and took a deep breath.

"So, I have to ask. Do you know how they found your blood at the scene of a murder?"

Paul cleared his throat. "No Nora, I have no clue!" He rose and walked to the window, parting the curtains and noting Mrs. Campbell had given up on her stakeout. He wheeled around and faced Nora. "I don't know how my blood was found at a murder scene." His heart raced as the image of glass shattering, and thick blood sliding down pointed shards to stain the beige carpet flooded his mind. And the eyes. He shook his head. Over the years his memory was reduced to her eyes. They continued to haunt him. The shame and guilt of leaving her like that stayed buried within. He turned away to stare out the window again.

Nora's touch startled him, as her arm settled around his waist. He draped his arm across her shoulders and she leaned her head against his chest.

"I know. I believe you. You couldn't hurt a fly." She gazed up into his face and a smile hinted at the corners of her mouth. "Okay, maybe a fly and definitely a spider, but that's one of the many reasons I love you."

Paul crumpled in her arms as tears slid down his cheeks. He needed to hear she believed him. Above all else, her faith in him was his greatest strength; his reason for getting clean. His reason for living.

CHAPTER FOUR
January 14, 2018

Sunday dawned bright and sunny, a rare occurrence for Vancouver in January. Paul lay still, watching Nora sleep. He knew she'd struggled to relax, as did he, but she'd finally succumbed to sleep and he didn't want to disturb her. He reached out to trace the ridge of her nose, stopping short of touching her. It dipped and rose at the tip, something he'd always loved. She appeared elf-like sleeping so soundly beside him, like she didn't have a care in the world. But she did. They did.

Her rhythmic breaths intoxicated him and he closed his eyes momentarily, listening intently to her soft inhales and slow exhales. How would he survive not laying beside her every night? He shuddered at the thought and Nora stirred. He held his breath and she fell back into the cadence deep sleep brings. Her brown hair touched by silver lay softly on the pillow. She'd cut it into a bob years ago. She still looked twenty-two to him. Other than a couple of crows feet, her skin was as flawless as the day they met. Nora and Zoe saved his life. If it weren't for them, he would've slipped into old habits time and again until it killed him.

They'd discussed the possibilities of the police investigation ad nauseam the night before. They decided not to call Zoe. They'd wait till they knew something concrete. Today they'd try to enjoy each other's company. Get some odd jobs done around the house, just in case. *Just in case.*

The sun peeked through the curtains and Paul carefully slid out of bed. He padded downstairs and into the kitchen where he started the coffee pot and pulled out the ingredients for pancakes from the cupboard and fridge. It was his normal Sunday routine. Normalcy seemed like such a luxury today.

*****

Tuesday morning, the phone rang. Detective Berstad's voice sounded apologetic on the other end of the phone. "We have the results. They're a match. We can pick you up, or you can come to the station."

Thoughts of Mrs. Campbell peering out of her living room window flashed through Paul's mind. He couldn't bring himself to speak. Berstad waited patiently on the other end of the phone. Paul cleared his throat. "Uh, I'll come in. Can you give me a couple of hours, though?" His words rang hollow. He hadn't figured out how his blood was found at the crime scene, but he'd steeled himself for this outcome.

There was a long pause and some muffled discussion in the background. Then Berstad cleared his throat. "Okay. If we don't see you here by one o'clock, we'll be coming for you."

Paul disconnected the call. He'd called in sick, but Nora went into work. He wandered into the kitchen and opened the dishwasher, loading the dishes from breakfast. He popped a tab into the dispenser and closed the door, selecting the normal cycle before climbing the stairs. He stopped in the doorway of the bedroom and stared at the bed. The bed he shared with Nora. The bed he may never crawl into again. His knees buckled, and he fell to the floor, sobbing. It wasn't fair to him or to her. And it certainly wasn't fair to Zoe. *Zoe.* The pit of his stomach churned. He had to call her. She knew nothing of his past. Perhaps if she had, she would've thought twice about putting her genetic information on a public site. Everyone these days heard about cases being solved by a relative's DNA posted to GENmatch.

He pulled his phone out of his pocket and lay on the floor, rolling to his back. The cool hardwood felt somehow comforting. He called April first. She agreed to pick him up and take him to the station. He dialled Zoe's number, but it went to voicemail. She rarely answered phone calls, and he hung up, not willing to leave a message. No longer able to put off the inevitable, he dialled Nora's office phone.

"Nora Giovanni, lab manager, how can I help you?"

If only she could help him. "It's me honey. The police called. I'm a match."

A sob escaped from the other end of the phone.

"Now listen. We'll fight this. I did nothing wrong. I've called April, and she'll take me to the station. At least they had the decency to give me the opportunity to turn myself in. Can you tell your colleagues you have a family emergency, and come home before I leave?" Paul's voice caught in his throat and he choked back tears.

An almost inaudible "Yes" travelled to Paul before the phone disconnected.

He texted Zoe, asking her to call. No response. He pulled himself up off the floor and strode into the ensuite. He brushed his teeth and set his toothbrush back in the holder next to Nora's pink one. Would he ever use that toothbrush again? He shook his head. *Stop thinking like this. You didn't do it.*

He wandered back into the bedroom and lay on the bed, waiting. What more was there to do? No sense packing anything. He slipped off his watchband and lay it on the nightstand. The glint of gold on his finger caught his eye. He hadn't taken his ring off since the day of their wedding. He turned it, debating. But he knew they'd take it from him and he'd rather it remained in the house than in lock-up at the prison. He twisted it and pulled, licking his finger to get it past his first knuckle. He held it up to the light. One small embedded diamond in a strip of white gold layered on yellow gold. He squeezed it in his fist and closed his eyes. Flashes of memories flooded his thoughts; lifting Nora's veil for their first long kiss as husband and wife, the doctor handing him the scissors to cut Zoe's cord, the look in Nora's eyes when she told him she didn't want to know anymore of his past. She knew enough and still loved him.

The gold chain holding a St. Christopher's medal slid to the side as he set his ring on the nightstand. He reached around his neck and undid the clasp. Nora had given that to him too, before they married. He leaned back into the pillow and waited. Soon he heard the key in the front door. He rose to his feet and met Nora racing down the hall. She flung herself into his arms, sobbing. Paul held her up and buried his face in her neck.

At last, he found his voice. "Nora, I tried calling Zoe and texted her to call me, but she hasn't responded. I'm sorry to leave this for you, but I don't want her to see it on the news. Can you…"

Nora stroked the back of his head. "I'll talk to her. It's okay."

They both heard it. A vehicle pulled into the drive. Paul straightened and placed his hands on Nora's arms, bringing them to her sides. "I've got to wash up." Nora nodded, a sob escaping from within.

"It's going to be okay. I promise."

*****

April Somersby emerged from the police station to a few reporters hanging around looking for juicy stories. Word was out.

"It's the defence lawyer!"

The crowd turned, and in unison thrust microphones in her direction. She cleared her throat and forced a smile. "This is a case of mistaken identity. My client is innocent, and we'll prove that."

She pushed her way through the crowd, ignoring the shouts, but one echoed in her head as she squeezed into her sports car and started the engine.

"How can DNA evidence be mistaken identity?"

How indeed.

HEATHER GRAY

CHAPTER FIVE
June 29, 1970

Paul gazed out of smeary windows from the fourth-floor apartment. The haze of a warm summer day floated upwards in ripples from roof tops. Tree leaves in Clark Park hung limp and listless. The air didn't move. Voices from below floated through the open window, and Paul struggled to get a better look. He knew the voices. A chill climbed his spine, and he shivered despite the stifling heat in the tiny apartment.

It would be a long summer. Joe, his best friend, begged him to join too. But his mother's words haunted him. "No child of mine will ever... Do you hear me?" She'd grabbed Paul's chin and forced him to look into her dark eyes. "Will ever join, hang out or even think about getting involved with a gang."

The hand on his jaw squeezed tighter, and he clenched his teeth.

"Tell me, Paul. Tell me you won't get mixed up in a gang. I don't work two jobs so you can join a gang. Tell me!"

Paul wiggled his jaw, and her grip loosened. "Promise."

"Promise what?" She stood in front of him, one hand on her hip, the other still holding his jaw.

"Promise I won't join a gang."

Her hand loosened, and she ruffled his hair. "That's my boy." She gave his cheek a playful pinch, and he winced. Why did she have to do that? It would be his twelfth birthday in a couple of days. He wasn't a kid anymore.

Paul shook away the memories from two days ago and focused on the voices below. But they faded as the gang strolled into the park and the red and black checked logger jackets disappeared into the trees below.

Oh, how he wanted to belong. Belong somewhere. Without Joe, he had no one to hang out with. His stomach churned, but he wasn't sure if it was from hunger or angst.

He opened the fridge and pulled out the milk jug. Then opened the cupboard, reaching to the back, hoping to find Captain Crunch. He'd tasted it at Joe's house once. The thought of that sugary goodness filled his mouth with saliva, but there was no Captain Crunch. Just Sunny Boy. His stomach grumbled, but Sunny Boy no longer felt adequate. He squeezed open the spout on the milk carton and took a swig before placing it back in the fridge. The bread bin held two stale pieces of Wonder bread, so he made himself a sugar sandwich, lathering on the butter and sprinkling sugar on top. Not Captain Crunch, but it would do.

Returning to the window, he noted a larger crowd gathered on the edge of the park, and he could hear the tinny rhythm of someone's transistor radio. He'd asked for one of those for his birthday, knowing they couldn't afford it. And he was right. Instead of a radio, that morning he'd unwrapped brown paper to find a striped T-shirt and pair of socks. He'd tried to mask his disappointment, but his mom's face reflected his, and she'd turned, mumbling an apology.

"I love the colours, Ma. And it will be great to wear a pair of socks without holes."

She smiled weakly, but the damage was done. Why hadn't he thought before he let his feelings show?

His dad raised his head from the couch to ask how they could afford that. Paul grabbed the shirt and shut himself in the bathroom before his dad decided they could take it back and get a refund. He heard the fight through the wall.

"Same way we can afford your whisky, I guess."

Paul winced, imagining his dad rising to his feet and smacking his mom across the face. But instead, the front door slammed. He breathed a sigh of relief and emerged from the bathroom.

"It fits perfectly Ma." He pulled down on the hem, trying to make it stretch a bit further over the waist of his pants.

She grabbed him and held him close. "Paul, you're a good boy."

He noted her purse on the counter. "You working today?"

"Yes, sorry. I know it's your birthday and the first day of summer vacation, but I told the Johnstons I'd get the house ready for their Canada Day celebrations. Sounds like they're going to have a big crowd." She turned and picked up her purse. "You and Joe getting together today?"

Paul hadn't told her about Joe's venture into the gang life. He didn't want her to forbid him to hang out with him, so he lied. "Oh yeah, he's invited me over for the afternoon."

"That's nice. Be good and mind your manners."

Her voice faded from his head as he watched Joe saunter into the group below. Everyone slapped him on the back. He was truly one of them now. Paul's throat tightened, and he wiped his eyes. *I don't need him, anyway.*

The plaid shirts moved into the park, and Paul turned on the TV. At least he had it for company. His dad had splurged one day and brought it home. He never heard where he got it, but assumed it wasn't at Woolworths. He didn't care. The TV would be his best friend over the summer. Turning the dial, he found *The Edge of Night*. There wasn't a lot of choice, so when his dad wasn't around, he watched the soaps.

A siren floated up into the apartment; the sound increased before suddenly stopping. Paul jumped to his feet and peered out the window. Two cops exited the patrol car and strode into the park. Paul knew they'd come out empty handed. The Clark Parkers would've been long gone after the racket they made. He stared into the park, wishing he had a group of friends who'd protect him. Even the threat of cops felt exciting. More exciting than *The Edge of Night*.

CHAPTER SIX
January 17, 2018

April Somersby strode into the visitation room, a black blazer over a white blouse tucked into her black pencil skirt. Every hair in its place in a tightly wound chignon. She carried a shopping bag and handed it to Paul.

"Sorry to keep you waiting. They took extra time going through the clothes I brought you." She rolled her eyes and let out a long-measured breath.

Paul peeked into the bag; dress pants, white shirt, sport coat, socks and dress shoes. He stared back at her; one eyebrow raised.

"I know, I know. You're not a dress-up kind of guy. But trust me, you need to make a good impression. Nora bought the clothes, and she has good taste."

Paul exhaled and set the bag on the floor beside him.

April placed her hands on the table. "Now, let's get to it. We don't have a lot of time before your bail hearing."

Paul raised his head and stared into April's eyes, inhaling and bracing himself for what he knew she'd say.

"Bail's difficult to get when you're up on a first-degree murder charge." Her eyes explored his.

A lump rose in his throat, and he coughed. "I can't stay in here. I have to get bail. And reasonable bail. We own our house and have some savings, but not a lot." Silence filled the room before Paul's fist hit the table. April jumped and the guard took a step toward them.

Paul leaned forward and stared into April's eyes. "Sorry. I'm just so frustrated. I have no idea how my blood could be at the crime scene."

April glanced at the guard and waved him off. "Okay, I hear you, but you need to get your emotions under control. An outburst in the courtroom won't do you any amount of good."

Paul nodded and straightened in his chair. "I know. I'm not an idiot." He glanced away from her stare. *What does she know about me?*

April cleared her throat. "Yes, well, for now, I need you to wear the clothes." She nodded toward the bag. "In the courtroom, sit up straight, don't show emotion, and leave the talking to me. Do you understand?"

Paul didn't need her treating him like a kid. Below the table he clenched his fists, but he nodded. "Understood."

April smiled. The rest of the words he wanted to say would have to remain unsaid. She was right. He needed to control himself.

"It'll only take a few minutes. When the prosecution provides their evidence in three or four weeks, we'll know what we're dealing with. During arraignment, after we've gone through the evidence, you'll make a plea. But I'm getting ahead of myself. Today it's important to make a good impression. Look the judge in the eye when she addresses you."

"I know, I know." Paul tried to keep the exasperation out of his voice, but April's raised eyebrows told him he wasn't doing a good job. He took another deep breath.

April raised her hand and continued. "And don't smile. Be as unemotional as you can without coming across as a cold-hearted bastard."

Paul broke into a grin. "So, don't be genuine, is what you're saying?"

April smiled back. "That's not what I'm saying. Here, try it with me." April sat up straight in her chair, staring at the table. She raised her head, all business. "Mr. Paul Giovanni, I grant you bail at $200,000."

Paul calmly stared into her eyes and nodded.

April slapped the table. "Perfect! The sincerity in your eyes was unmistakable. Act just like that in the courtroom."

Paul shook his head. "I didn't fake the sincerity, you know. I need bail."

April leaned back and studied Paul's face. There was a pause before she responded. "DNA evidence is pretty compelling, Paul. Prepare yourself for the likelihood you won't get bail. But I'll do my best to plead with the judge to grant it. How much could you afford?"

Paul sighed and tilted his head back, staring at the ceiling before leaning forward again. "We could re-mortgage the house and come up with five hundred thousand dollars. I'm sixty years old and can't spend the rest of my life in jail, especially for a crime I never committed. I need you to believe me when I say I'm not guilty."

April leaned forward. "Trust me, Paul, I always believe my clients. If I didn't, I couldn't represent them. I also believe the judicial system works, and I'm good at my job. While I can't guarantee an outcome, I promise I'll do everything in my power to ensure the outcome is in your favour."

"Thank you." Paul stood and extended his hand toward her.

April grasped it firmly. "You're welcome. Now let's get this bail hearing behind us. Get changed, and I'll see you shortly."

He grabbed the bag and traipsed back to his cell with a guard in tow.

*****

Paul paced back and forth in his new clothes. Nora had done well. They fit perfectly. He reached into his pant's pockets and felt a small piece of paper. Turning his back to the door, he unfolded the note. *I'm so sorry. I love you, Dad.*

His knees buckled, and he lowered himself to the bunk. He hadn't talked to Nora, but knew she would've talked to Zoe by now. She must have flown home. Nora would need the support, but he wished Zoe had stayed at school. The second semester was just underway.

So, she knew, and she still loved him. He held the paper to his heart, closed his eyes, and concentrated on his breathing. Tears stung the back of his eyelids, but he fought them back. He coughed and flexed his neck. He couldn't break down now.

"Giovanni! Time to go."

His eyes snapped open, and he shoved the paper in his pocket. This was it. The start of a journey he'd rather not take.

HEATHER GRAY

CHAPTER SEVEN
July 7, 1970

"What have we here?"

Paul glanced up and realized he'd walked too far. When his father's alcoholic rage sent him into the streets, he bided time till his dad either passed out or left the apartment. And so, he wandered down side streets, searching the ground for lost coins. One day he'd even found a dollar bill, but not today.

Paul froze. Without thinking, he'd walked into Riley Park. Four guys stood in front of him, hands on their hips. One swung some kind of baton, like the one the cops carried.

He backed up a step before turning to run. But another member blocked his escape, sticking out his leg before Paul could register what was happening. His face hit the sidewalk, and he rolled to his side onto the grass. Blood streaked the back of his hand when he wiped it across his face, and his nose dripped blood. Laughter surrounded him, then the baton came out of nowhere. He tried to roll away, but it landed across his stomach. He doubled over and gasped for air.

"Get up, you sissy. Where're you from and why're you in our territory?"

Paul crawled to his knees and stood; blood dripped onto his shirt. His birthday shirt. *Ma will have a fit.*

"Sorry, I wasn't paying attention. I didn't mean to come into your park."

"Where you come from?" The kid with the baton jerked his head upwards and smacked the stick rhythmically into his left hand.

"That way." Paul pointed toward home, then dropped his hand when the boy's face morphed into a smirk.

"You one of the Clark Parkers?" The rhythm of the baton sped up.

Paul paused. Would it be better to lie and say he was. He studied the face in front of him. "No, no, I don't belong to any gang. Please, just let me go. I didn't mean to cause trouble."

The kid with the baton stepped closer. Paul stared at the ground. The baton's rhythm stopped, but he saw the shadow of it being twirled and shoes came into his peripheral vision.

"Tell you what, kid. You can go, but first empty your pockets, and give us all you have."

"I got nothin'. I swear." He reached into his pockets and turned them out, glancing at the kid's face in front of him.

"Get out of here. You're a nobody." He waved the baton toward the park entrance.

Laughter followed him as he turned and ran to the edge of the park. How could he be so stupid? He knew better than to wander into Riley Park territory. Leaving with only a few bruises and a bloody nose was sheer luck.

After that day, Paul paid more attention. Days in the apartment were long, and he wandered the streets only when the threat at home was greater than what the street offered. So far, he'd escaped the wrath of his drunken father too.

A gang could protect him on the streets, but his mom didn't understand. Joe probably had something to do with the Clark Parkers leaving him alone. But he was fair game for other gangs. He needed protection.

If he wasn't part of the Clark Parkers, he was at risk. And he couldn't stay cooped up in the apartment all summer. Everyday when the Clark Park gang met across the street there'd be high fives and slaps on the back. They'd laugh and rib each other. They were good guys. He knew he was right about them, and his mom had it all wrong.

The mid-July sun created sweltering heat inside the apartment the day he made his way down to the street and waited, kicking rocks and counting cars passing by. A police car pulled up and slowed. Paul turned and walked along the sidewalk in the opposite direction. They pulled away from the curb, and he returned to the park entrance.

Some checkered shirts walked toward him. His heart pulsed in his ears. He glanced up at his apartment, glad his mom wasn't home to see him defy her wishes, but also wishing she was, and would pull him back up to the apartment by his ear. His knees weakened. This had to be the right decision. He couldn't stand being cooped up all summer, and the Riley Parkers needed to understand they wouldn't bully him again.

"Hey kid, what ya doin' hanging around our park?"

Paul peered into an unforgiving face, swallowed and straightened, wishing he was big for his age. "I want to join your gang."

He glanced around, searching for Joe.

"Oh yeah? And what makes you think you're good enough to join?"

Paul swallowed again. "I fought off the Riley Parker's?" The squeak that interrupted his voice these days snuck in. His face burned, and he reverted to a lame kid who didn't belong in a gang. But he continued to stare into the face opposite him.

"The Riley Parker's, eh? What do ya think, boys?" He turned to the three boys standing behind him.

Paul stepped forward. "Oh, and I know a Clark Parker.

The taller boy turned back toward him. "And who would that be?"

"Joe, Joe Walters." The squeak snuck out again and his voice trailed off.

The face broke out into a broad-faced grin, and Paul exhaled. "Well, that makes it official." He slapped Paul on the back, just like he'd seen them do all summer from his apartment vantage point. "Better come with us."

Paul grinned, straightened, and followed close behind. His stomach churned, as he pushed his mother's words away. She didn't understand. She knew nothing. To survive Vancouver's east side, he needed to be part of something bigger than himself.

HEATHER GRAY

CHAPTER EIGHT
January 18, 2018

"To April Somersby, Vancouver's newest celebrity lawyer." Her friends raised their glasses, expressions shining with admiration.

April lowered her head, face burning. "Too funny, guys. So far, DNA evidence places my client at the scene, and I've got nothing. A celebrity for all the wrong reasons."

She'd taken the case, because a high-profile cold case could do wonders for her career. Even if they didn't win, her name would be all over the media.

April tipped up her wineglass and let the red liquid laced with cherry and oak notes slide down her throat. This was likely the last time she'd socialize for a while with the court case eating up spare moments. She loved the lawyers she worked with, but they were her only friends. And they discussed work even in their off-time.

Her gaze rested beyond Rick and Joan across the table from her, and the conversation faded. A man sitting at the bar caught her eye. He smiled, raised his glass, and winked. *Did he really just wink at me?* April turned her attention to the table behind her hoping, and yet not hoping, his stare and especially his wink was for someone else.

But the table behind sat empty. She faced forward, and he continued to stare and smile. Not a creepy smile. A Tom Cruise smile. April smiled thinly and glanced away before taking another sip.

What am I doing? She set her glass down and pulled her attention back to the table and the conversation. Rick spouted off about some guy who wandered into his office, wanting him to represent him in a lawsuit against Walmart. The table erupted into laughter. April didn't know what was funny, but she joined in. She glanced back at the bar. The stranger had vanished.

Damn! As weird as the encounter may have seemed, there was something about him that intrigued her. She took one last swallow of wine, emptying her glass, and shook her head when Rick reached for the bottle. "With lots of work ahead of me starting tomorrow, I don't need a headache and a fuzzy brain. Think it's time for me to go." April opened her wallet and set a couple of twenties on the table. "This should cover my share."

She rose, stealing a glance at the bar, but 'Tom Cruise' had vanished. "See you guys at the office." With a wave, she strode toward the door, stopping abruptly, her breath catching in her throat. Leaning against the door frame, he watched her, his grin somehow magnetic. She shouldered her purse and continued straight toward him, ignoring the flutter in her stomach. Getting picked up in a bar wasn't something she did, but she wanted to hear what he had to say.

"Well, hello April Somersby." The stranger extended his hand toward her.

She smiled and took his hand, making sure her grip was firmer than his. *How does he know my name?*

As if sensing her question, he cleared his throat and let her hand drop. "I saw you on television earlier, and when your friends toasted a few minutes ago, I realized it was you. I'm David Windsor, and no, I'm not a creepy stalker or someone needing a lawyer. You just seem like someone I'd like to get to know."

Despite being in her late forties, and having heard every pickup line, April's face burned school-girl hot. But she stood her ground, refusing to lower her gaze.

"Do you always approach women you're attracted to?" April stared into his blue eyes, noting they weren't the usual blue-green combination, but a brilliant blue framed by long black lashes. Her heart quickened, despite trying to put this guy back in his place.

There was a pause before David responded. "I guess I'd have to say yes to that. You're the first woman I've been attracted to enough to approach in a bar." The big grin spread across his face again and his eyes twinkled. April had to admit she loved twinkling eyes.

"Quite the pickup lines you've got. I'll have to give you that." April glanced back at her table of friends. They hadn't noticed she lingered in the bar. She stepped forward reaching for the door.

David's arm reached for the door as well, causing her to pause. "Listen, I want to get to know you better. Can we grab a table and have a drink together?" His eyebrows raised, making his eyes impossibly larger.

"Sorry, I just told my friends I was heading home. I've got a big day tomorrow." The words spilled out and yet April felt regret in her gut as soon as she said them. Wasn't she looking for a relationship? Someone to spend time with that wasn't part of her office group?

"We could go somewhere else if you're worried about what your friends might think."

April cleared her throat. "No, that's not it. I just really need to get home." April pursed her lips. *Why don't I want to get to know this guy. Am I sabotaging my potential for a relationship?* She was tired of being alone. She let go of the door and peered up into David's eyes. "Wait, you know what?"

David grinned and chimed in immediately. "What?"

"Maybe we could chat for a few minutes." A shiver ran up her spine and she glanced at her friends, deep in conversation and laughter. *What am I doing?*

"I really appreciate that." His eyes searched hers. Then she felt a gentle hand on her back, guiding her to a booth at the back of the bar.

They slid in across from each other.

"I don't normally do this." April gripped her hands tightly in her lap, suddenly feeling like a teenager and chiding herself for being so weak.

"Neither do I. Honestly, this isn't like me at all. You caught my eye before I realized you were the person I saw on TV. I'm curious about why you'd take that case on, but that's not the reason I want to get to know you."

April couldn't figure him out. He seemed genuine. But was she being naïve? What were his motives?

The server approached, placing cardboard coasters in front of them. "What can I get you?"

David gestured toward April.

"A cosmopolitan please."

"And I'll have a Glenfiddich, neat."

The server nodded and wandered off.

"Cosmopolitan? Weren't you drinking wine?"

"So, you're observant, too. Can't a girl mix things up?" She grinned across the table at him. The blond hair with subtle grey at the temples, and a chiseled jaw. He was a lot to like.

"Absolutely. Happy to see a lady mix it up."

Was that a wink again? Something deep down felt unsettling. That shiver crept up her spine again.

"Sorry, will you excuse me?" April grabbed her purse and walked briskly down the hall. In the washroom, she studied her reflection. *Really? Are you going to walk out on this guy because he winks?* She stared at a woman at the top of her game; fit, independent, and in a career, she not only loved but excelled at. Did she need a relationship right now?

She stood back, took a deep breath, and walked out of the bathroom and out of the bar.

Regret rose in her throat as she turned the key in the ignition. She swallowed it down and threw her car into drive and pointed herself toward the freeway.

*****

The next day Paul sat across the table from April. The bail hearing had not gone well. Not well at all. The judge didn't even entertain bail, citing the seriousness of a first-degree murder charge.

"What do you want to know?" Paul took a deep breath, trying to calm his nerves.

"Anything from your past you think may be relevant to the case." April sat poised with pen and paper.

Paul cleared his throat. "Well, I'm sure you've done your homework and know all about my past. Why don't you tell me what you know?"

"Sorry, that's not how it works." April sat back in her chair, resting the pen on the table. "I need to hear it from you. I try not to look into things until I hear it from my clients first."

Paul noted the exasperation in her voice. He didn't mean to make it hard for her. Shame made it difficult to talk about his past. "Okay, well, I'm sure you know I was a member of a street gang in the 70s."

"The Clark Park gang, is that correct?" April picked up the pen and started jotting notes.

Paul stared at the pen and April laid it down again.

"Listen, Paul, I need to take notes. I'm your lawyer. I'll hold everything you say in strictest confidence. The more you tell me, the better prepared I'll be to defend you. Now, you were a member of the Clark Park gang, right?" She picked up the pen and sat poised, waiting for Paul's response.

A long silence hung between them before Paul raised his head to meet April's eyes. "I joined the Clark Park gang when I was twelve."

"Twelve? That's awfully young, isn't it?"

Paul rolled his eyes and sighed. "No, in those days, it was quite common. Probably still is today, too. My mom worked all the time and my dad drank. I joined a gang to protect myself from other gangs, because I needed to leave the house to avoid my dad. It wasn't safe on the street unless you had protection. The Clark Parkers gave me that, and so much more." Paul stopped and watched his life bleed across the notepad in front of him.

April glanced up. "Go on. Did you get in trouble with the police?"

Paul laughed and nodded. "You could say that, but you have to understand. The gangs back then weren't the same as today. Guns were scarce, and it was petty thievery, mostly. Televisions, jewellery, that sort of thing. We weren't killers, and we didn't set out to hurt anyone, but of course if they crossed our turf, we'd stand up for ourselves." Paul studied April.

She wrote in her notepad, not seeming to notice he'd paused. The pen stopped as she flipped the page and then continued to write. "Sorry, just give me a second."

Paul placed a hand on his thigh to stop his knee from bouncing up and down. It was a nervous response he needed to learn to control.

"Okay, thanks for your patience. So, were you ever arrested?"

Paul grinned, recalling the number of times he graced the backseat of a cruiser. "Yeah, more times than I can count. But lucky for me, the charges never materialized. Being so young, I was too much paperwork for them. At least that's how I interpret it. Some members used to call me 'Soap' on account of my ability to slip through the police system. It got so they'd send me in to places first, because they knew if I got caught it wouldn't be as serious as them getting caught." Paul rose and strode over to the water fountain as April scribbled and flipped pages.

"What years were you part of the gang?"

Paul sat down. "July 1970 to November 1972."

"So, a little over two years. But that was twenty years before the murder you're being accused of. What's the connection there?"

Paul swallowed. "Nothing. You said you wanted me to talk about my past and that's what I'm doing. I thought being a former member of a street gang might be relevant to the prosecution. It doesn't paint me in the best light."

"True. But what you were up to in 1994, when the murder happened." April stared into Paul's eyes. She flexed her authoritative muscle, and Paul felt it.

"I don't recall." Paul returned her stare, unblinking.

April tapped the pen on the pad of paper. "Okay, Paul. That's not helping me and it's certainly not helping you. I need you to recall what you were doing on April 17, 1994. Where were you living? Were you working? Did you have a girlfriend? Did you have any gang ties, old or new? You've had plenty of time to think about this."

Paul stared back. "Like I said, I don't recall."

April slammed the notepad shut and rose from the table. "Okay, we're done for today. If you won't help me, I can't help you."

Paul remained sitting as she buzzed, and a guard opened the door to let her out. She never glanced back at him, not even once. He slammed the table with his fist. "Damn it!" His voice echoed off the cement floor and walls.

"Whoa there, cowboy. Do I need to call in additional guards to take you back to your cell?

Paul clenched his fists. Big Ed stared down at him as he smacked a baton into his left hand. Paul crossed his arms in front of his chest, recalling what a baton felt like when slammed into his gut. He took a deep breath and unclenched his fists, letting his arms drop to his sides. "No need, I'm fine. Take me back."

As his cell door closed and latched, his anger swelled again. He hated needing anyone, but he needed April Somersby.

His mind flooded with memories he'd suppressed for the past twenty-four years. Memories that held shame and guilt, remorse and panic. Memories he couldn't speak about to anyone.

CHAPTER NINE
January 20, 2018

The National News silently lit up the TV screen behind the bar. The scrolling words caught his attention. *Paul Giovanni denied bail.* "Must be a slow news day." The gentleman loosened his tie and took a sip, watching the tawny liquid eddy before setting it back down.

The bartender glanced at the screen, then turned to the man seated at the bar. "Why'd yah say that?"

Save for the two of them, the man noted the bar was empty. The bartender lifted the cocktail menu and wiped the bar, shaking out the cloth before setting the menu back down and pausing to study the man in front of him.

"They're still reporting about no bail for the guy charged in that cold case murder. The bail hearing was a couple of days ago."

"Guess it's a big deal. I remember the murder, and how it rocked the city, setting off gang wars." The bartender scrubbed at something stuck to the granite surface of the bar. "Guess you aren't from around here?"

"No, not here." He cleared his throat. "Why were there gang wars?" He took another sip, swirling his glass as he stared at the TV.

"At the time, they speculated it was a contract killing. The woman was a kid in the seventies when her brothers entered gang life. In the eighties and nineties, she got caught up with other gangs dealing drugs. I guess she was a pretty big deal with a gang at the time of her death. They swore to avenge her death, but no one took credit for the murder. This Giovanni guy they've got in custody makes little sense, but DNA doesn't lie. As far as I know, he lived a pretty clean life. Doesn't seem like the contract killer type."

The man smiled and cleared his throat. "And what type is the contract killer type?"

"I guess I don't know. Never met one that I know of. Never can tell what secrets people keep, I guess."

"They must think he's a serious contender for the role. No bail? Now, that's brutal."

The bartender laid down his cloth and stopped polishing the spigots. "I suppose so, but I suspect that's pretty common for a first-degree murder charge."

"But, like you said, he's lived a clean life; quiet, kept his nose clean. Is he a threat to society?"

"I hear yah, but it's getting harder and harder to tell the good guys from the bad guys."

He downed the last of the liquor in his glass and pushed it toward the barkeep.

The bartender paused and sighed. "Can I get you anything else? Want a top up?"

"No, no, I'm good. So, you think it's a pretty closed case. The guy's done for?"

The bartender shook out his cloth again. "Well, don't you? The DNA doesn't give the defence any wiggle room. He was at the scene of the crime and since it was in her apartment, I'd say that's pretty conclusive evidence."

The man smiled weakly and nodded. "Hey, thanks for keeping me company. I suspect you'll be able to close up when I leave." He stood, readjusted his tie and left a five-dollar bill on the counter. "Again, thanks for your time."

The bartender slid the five in his jeans pocket. "Have a good evening."

The man strolled across the lobby and pushed the button for the elevator. He knew how to blend in when he had to so no one would remember he was ever there.

The elevator doors opened, and a couple strolled out without a glance in his direction. He passed the key fob over the sensor and pressed the button labelled the penthouse. A brunette entered before the elevator door closed. He brushed a piece of lint off his lapel.

The elevator stopped on the 18th floor and she exited. He stared at her legs as they disappeared around the corner before the doors slid shut. But he wasn't in town for that sort of fun. It was important to keep things clean and focused. He had a job to do. No mixing business with pleasure.

The elevator opened into his suite. At least it was his for now. He stepped out and slipped off his jacket, hanging it in the walk-in closet off the bedroom. He changed into khakis and a polo shirt and strode onto the balcony. The city lights twinkled, a bus roared by somewhere below, and seagulls squawked into the night. The music from the bar across the street, the one he should have gone to instead of the hotel bar, floated up to his balcony. He sat on a patio chair, glancing at his phone. No new messages. A sigh escaped his lips as he returned the phone to his pocket. Sleep was a rare commodity. As soon as his head hit that pillow, he'd be wide awake. Settling in, he leaned against the back of his chair and closed his eyes. He'd never quite gotten used to this lonely life.

CHAPTER TEN
January 22, 2018

Paul tapped the table, slouched down in the chair, feet sprawled in front of him. The door buzzed, and he straightened, clasping his hands in his lap. The guard held the door open, and April Somersby walked through, her heels clicking sharply on the sealed cement floor.

"Hi Paul, how're you doing?" She sat in the chair on the opposite side of the table.

Paul eyed her demeanour. She didn't seem upset. "Can't complain."

"Well, I can tell you I don't hear that too often. Glad things are okay." She pulled a pen and notepad from her bag, before hanging it over the back of her chair. "So, Paul, I've given you a couple of days to think about things. Are you ready to talk about what you were doing in 1994, around April 17th?

Paul took his time. Some days it felt like shame filled every cell of his body. Talking about his life wasn't easy, but he nodded.

"Okay then, let's get started." April sat poised with her pen hovering over the notepad.

Paul stared at the table, unable to form words.

April sighed and leaned back in her chair. "Okay, Paul, let's start with where you worked."

Silence filled the room, but April sat still, waiting for him to fill the void.

Paul squirmed in his seat, then sat forward and placed his hands flat on the table. "I was unemployed."

April waited for more explanation, but none came. "How did you become unemployed?"

"They fired me." Paul stared into her eyes, unwavering.

"Okay... why?"

"The heavy-duty mechanic's job was a good one, and I was good at it. But I started drinking, then taking drugs. Nothing big, pot and a little cocaine."

"So, they fired you because the alcohol and drugs interfered with your job?" April jotted down a few notes.

Paul noted she wasn't trying to capture everything like last time. "You could say that." He clenched his teeth against the tension mounting in the room.

April cleared her throat. "Okay, so you were unemployed. Where were you living?" April tapped her notepad with the pen.

"Nowhere and everywhere. Truth be told, anywhere."

April set her pen down and shook her head.

"I was homeless, and remember little from then. It was rainy and cool on the streets. I slept in doorways and under trees. Sometimes I found a bed in a shelter or laid in a gutter. And sometimes I rented an apartment for a week or two if my gambling paid off."

"Do you remember anything about the days around April 17 of 1994?" She picked up her pen and scribbled a few notes.

"I barely knew it was 1994 back then." Paul lowered his eyes and traced graffiti embedded in the tabletop with his right index finger.

"Paul, I need you to think harder. This is important. Did you ever stay with a friend? Is there anyone who can help you remember where you were?"

"No, I had no one. My foster parents didn't know where I was. As far as they knew, I'd dropped off the face of the earth. I feel bad about that. Hurting them was never my intention. They died in a car accident in 1995. I saw it on the news. Hadn't talked to them for years." Paul leaned back in his chair.

"Did you go to rehab? How'd you get clean?"

"I'd have to credit my wife for that. I mean, I went to rehab, more than once. But every time I got out, I'd fall back into it. But then I met Nora. She was reason enough to give it all up."

April smiled and leaned forward. "When was that?"

"We met in May 1994, and married two years later." Paul's jaw relaxed into a smile as he thought about life back then. "We weren't planning to have kids, but when Zoe came along, well, we wondered why we hadn't done it sooner. For me, I guess it was because I had such a rough childhood. My mom tried, but she had my dad to deal with."

"I've heard kids will change your life" April shook her head and scrawled something on her paper, turning the page and continuing on the next.

Paul waited for April to continue the conversation.

She raised her head. "So, you met your wife shortly after Lori Trembley died. Does that spark any memories of where you were on April 17, 1994?

Paul bit his lip. He'd said too much. *Damn.*

April leaned back in her chair and let out an exasperated sigh. "Okay, Paul, let's back up a bit. When did you end up in the foster system?"

Paul's eyes narrowed, and he sat consumed by thoughts. What would his foster parents have thought of him now? They tried so hard, but he was just born to be screwed up. They never gave up on him. And neither did Nora. He let out a sigh. Nora. Did she believe him? How long would it take until she didn't?

"Um, I entered the system in November 1972. My foster family kept me until I turned eighteen and could live on my own."

April leaned forward and flipped another page in her notebook. "So, what happened to your parents?"

Paul cleared his throat. "Murder/suicide."

April stared at him, the crease between her eyebrows visible. "You need to explain that one to me, Paul."

Paul's eyes widened. "Oh, so you think I was involved? Damn. Are you sure you want to represent me? Seems like you aren't exactly on my side."

April placed her hand on the table between them and leaned forward. "Now listen here. I need to know all of the skeletons in your closet. It doesn't mean I blame you for them. But I can assure you the prosecution will. If you can't take my questions, you won't be taking the stand. I don't know who will defend you, Paul. You might be your only hope."

Paul gazed at the ceiling and inhaled. She was right. He was his only hope. "Dad murdered Mom and then committed suicide. If I'd been home, maybe I could have stopped him."

"Or maybe you'd be dead too. Look, Paul, it sounds like you've had more than your share of trauma. You've made a nice life for yourself after leaving that world. Try to hang onto that."

Paul leaned forward, clenching and unclenching his fists. "I made it out, and now I'm sucked back in. I thought my past was behind me, but the police can't leave me alone."

"Sorry Paul, remember I'm on your side. We'll fight this, but I need more details. Friends, acquaintances, enemies?"

Paul's face clouded over and his jaw clenched. April's perfect hair and perfect outfit and the way she sat up straight, no signs of the years taking their toll on her, sickened him. She likely grew up with money and attended only the best schools with the most well-behaved kids. She didn't have a clue what it was like to have lived and survived like he did. His anger at the unfairness of the world, bubbled over and he leaned forward, controlling his tone and his words as best he could. "I had no friends, acquaintances, or enemies."

April closed her notepad and rose. "Okay, Paul, we both know that's not true. We'll stop for today."

April pressed the buzzer, and the door opened. The click of her heels faded down the hall. Paul rose, and a guard led him back to his cell. He crawled onto the bunk, and the door clanged shut. He rolled onto his side and faced the wall, kicking it in frustration.

*****

April stormed out of the prison and sat in her car, head resting on the steering wheel. Damn him, why wouldn't he help her defend him? *Maybe he is guilty.*

But there was something about him that appealed to her sense of fairness. He'd had a tough life, and he'd pulled himself out of it. But was it a murder that gave him the jolt he needed to straighten out?

She turned the key, and the engine roared to life. She passed through the prison gates and onto the freeway. The clock blinked 5:20. A quiet apartment didn't appeal to her, and her mind drifted back to the bar and David. Maybe she'd been too quick to judge. But she had no way of contacting him. She hadn't stuck around long enough to exchange phone numbers. Maybe he'd be at the bar again? Just one drink, then she'd go home.

She pulled into The Sticky Wicket and flipped down the visor, adjusting her hair and applying fresh lipstick. Black rings framed her eyes. Going home to sleep would be better. She nodded to her reflection, vowing she'd only stay for one.

Loud conversations greeted her as she opened the door. She paused, letting her eyes adjust to the dim lighting before striding up to the bar. A quick scan revealed David wasn't there.

"What'll it be?" A coaster appeared in front of her and she glanced up into the bartender's face. "Australian Cab Sav, nine ounces please."

A familiar voice resonated from behind her. "Starting with the big glass? Must have been a tough day."

April inhaled as he placed a hand on her back before perching on the stool beside her. Shivers ran up her spine. She glanced in his direction and felt the heat rise in her cheeks. Did she think he'd be happy to see her after she dumped him the other night? His Tom Cruise grin stared back at her. Maybe he wasn't upset.

"You could say that." She grinned and lowered her gaze. "Hey, I'm sorry I did the disappearing act the other night. I just needed to get home." It was lame, and she knew it. She raised her eyes to meet his.

"Hey, no problem. Glad we bumped into each other again. I shouldn't have insisted we have a drink. You were ready to head home. My apologies." He winked at her again.

April cringed. *What is it with this guy?* "Look, can I be honest?"

His smile faded. "Why do I feel you're ready to walk out the door again? Please, be honest."

"This might seem ridiculous, but I hate it when men wink at me. It makes me feel somehow like less of a person. Winks don't win me over." April wasn't sure what she expected him to do, but he surprised her with a chuckle and he reached for her hand.

"I have a small tick, don't even know when I'm doing it. Honest, I'm not trying to wink at you, it just happens. My apologies if it offends you. Please forgive me. If I could stop it, I would."

April grinned back and squeezed his hand. "Oh, I'm so sorry."

"No worries, forgive me?"

"Forgive you? It's you who needs to forgive me. Maybe we could start over?" She pulled back her hand and then reached out to him. "Hi, I'm April Somersby, wink hater, and you are?"

"David Windsor, involuntary winker. Pleased to make your acquaintance. Sounds like we're a match made in heaven." He gripped her hand.

They burst into fits of laughter. The glass of wine appeared and David raised his glass of Scotch. "To friendship!"

April felt a warm glow creep into her cheeks. A friend was just what she needed. "To friendship." She touched her glass to his. The warmth of the liquid felt good, but her stomach protested. "Would you mind if we order something to eat? I just realized I haven't eaten since this morning."

"Sounds like a great idea. Why don't we grab a table?"

David led her away from the bar, choosing a table off to the side, before waving over a waitress and ordering an appetizer.

"So, do you just hang out here every day, or why're you here today?"

David shifted in his seat. "It's embarrassing, actually. I've been back a few times since we met. Not because I like the place, although it's cozy, but because I hoped to bump into you again. I've never done this before, but you intrigue me. I hoped I'd find you again, and please don't think I'm creepy?"

"Well, since we're confessing, I have to say I came here hoping to run into you, too. So, if you're creepy, I guess I am, too." April couldn't quit staring at his chiseled features. He seemed like the real deal. The total package. But she knew to tread carefully after her history with men. "So, what is it you do, David?"

"Don't judge me by my profession, okay?"

April chuckled. "Promise."

"I'm an investment broker."

April tilted her head. "Why would you be ashamed of that?"

"Oh, not ashamed, just so many people associate it with greedy and stuffy. I hope I'm neither of those." He adjusted the collar on his shirt.

April had to admit, that profession did conjure up those stereotypes. "So, if those adjectives don't describe you, what does?" She ran her finger around the base of her wine glass.

"Oh, tough question. I'm an introvert who likes my alone time, but I also like to get out with friends, meet new people, have fun. I wear a suit a lot, but I don't think that makes me stuffy. I prefer fashionable. And I volunteer for different organizations like the Food Bank and United Way, and I run for causes to raise money. So, I hope that makes me philanthropic. How about you? What floats your boat?" David moved the cocktail menu, making room for the appetizer.

The waitress set the charcuterie board on the table between them. "Anything else I can get you? Another drink?"

David looked at April and raised his eyebrows.

"Yes, another Cab Sav, please. Make it a six ounce this time."

"Another Glenfiddich, neat, please. And a jug of water?"

The server left them alone. April's stomach growled, and she reached for some prosciutto and cheese.

"Sorry to just dive in, but I'm starving." Usually on a first dinner date, she barely ate. But her comfort level with David surprised her. Maybe it was because he called them friends. There was no pretense of a date. They were just two people meeting over drinks and appetizers. It had been a long time since she'd felt this comfortable around anyone she didn't work with.

"No need to apologize." He sat back and stared at her; his charismatic grin pasted to his face.

"Aren't you hungry?" She reached for her glass and took a sip of wine. "Maybe I'm starving, but this is delicious."

"I ate before you came in, but I'll pick at it, not to worry." David raised his glass to his lips, then set it back down and leaned forward. "But you've skirted my question. What floats your boat?"

April caught the twinkle in his eye. He was interested in getting to know her. "To be honest, I'm obsessive, especially with work. I enjoy digging into evidence and finding discrepancies to help my clients. So, I guess you could say puzzles float my boat."

"But as a defence attorney, don't you worry about getting guilty clients off? Why do you defend people who have done terrible things?" David reached for a few cashews.

"It's the adage 'everyone's innocent until proven guilty' I look at my job as holding the prosecutor accountable to do their job. If they can't prove guilt beyond a reasonable doubt, it's on them, not me." April clasped her wine glass and sat back in her chair before raising it to her lips. The hunger edge eased.

"True. A good way to look at it. Is that why you've taken on this momentous case? I mean, they've got DNA evidence. How do you fight that?"

"I haven't seen their evidence yet. I'm expecting it soon though. With a cold case, the disclosure by the prosecution happens quicker than usual."

"Do you think they've got more than DNA evidence?" David reached for a piece of cheese and bit into it.

April shook her head and cleared her throat. "I can't talk about the case, but there's always a crack. Every case has something. I just need to find it."

"I'm so sorry, didn't mean to pry into your case. It's just that the media has decided he's guilty." David leaned back in his chair.

"And there's the problem right there. They've declared him guilty before a trial has even started, so where is the justice in that?" April felt her face flush. She knew her Libra tendencies were coming out; the powerful need for fairness to prevail.

David raised his glass. "Here, here. I concur. I think I'm liking you more and more, April Somersby."

He winked at her, and this time April smiled. She thought the same thing about him.

CHAPTER ELEVEN
May 20, 1972

Paul shifted his weight from foot to foot as he stood beside the open door. He peered outside. No sirens, no nosy neighbours. He took a deep breath and exhaled slowly. The sound of drawers sliding open in the kitchen escaped down the hall. Once they were done with the main floor, they'd head upstairs.

"What the hell's going on here?"

Paul stared at a man about his dad's age, standing at the top of the stairs. His white tank-top stretched across an enormous belly, and his boxer shorts hung to his knees. Time stood still. He'd checked the place out and no one was home. He was positive. How had he missed someone this big? Where was he when Paul snuck through the basement window and crept through every room? He'd checked every single room. The large man's eyes bulged, his face glowed red. His arms were the size of fence posts, for Christ's sake.

"Run!" His voice squeaked. "Run!" He repeated, this time as loudly as he could muster.

The man lunged down the stairs.

Someone grabbed him and dragged him out the door. He stumbled and landed in a heap beside the sidewalk. There was a tug on the back of his mackinaw, so he wiggled out of it, found his footing and booked it for the park. The gang would be furious. It was up to him to secure the place, and he failed. Three boys ran ahead. Someone was missing. There were five, including himself, on this job. They were supposed to find cash and maybe some jewellery. Nothing big this time, but if there was a TV, maybe they'd come back with a vehicle for transport. There was always a process. Stake out, break in, grab the small stuff, note the big stuff, and get out. Sometimes they grabbed food too, but they always took it to go. No sense taking more risks than necessary. The police were onto them and doing more day patrols in the area. It was getting trickier.

Paul eased up, trying to catch his breath before meeting the rest at the predetermined clearing in the middle of Clark Park.

"What the hell happened, Soap? You said the place was clear?"

"I swear guys, I checked it out, every room. I don't know how I missed him."

"And where's Joe?"

Paul glanced back in the direction he came. There was no sign of Joe. He ran a hand through his hair. "Shit man, I'm so sorry. If he's arrested, this is on me. I take full responsibility."

"Damn right it's on you." Al stepped toward Paul; fists clenched at his side.

Jack stepped between the two and held up his hand. "Okay, Al, that's enough. The kid admitted it's his fault, and we've all made mistakes. Take a step back."

Al shook his head, but retreated, shaking out his fists, still glaring at Paul. Then his gaze shifted to behind Paul, and a grin spread across his face. Joe sauntered up the walk, clutching a checkered shirt in his left hand.

"Here you go." He threw the shirt at Paul and then burst into laughter. "I would love to have seen your face, man. You thought I was the old codger. I was just trying to help you up, but you wiggled out of your shirt as slick as a whore wiggling out of a silk blouse. Gotta give you credit, you know how to get away."

The gang burst into peels of laughter. Now that they were all safe, Paul had to admit it was funny.

"Sorry guys, I swear it won't happen again. I've learned my lesson to be thorough."

Joe slapped him on the back. "We've all made mistakes, live and learn." Joe turned to the group. "So, did anybody score anything? I came away empty handed except for Soap's shirt."

Jim held up a bag of apples. No one else had anything. They divided up the spoils and lay on the grass, recovering.

Paul broke the silence. "So, what's next?"

Jim took a bite of his apple, spittle dripping down his chin, before he wiped it away with his sleeve. "The Asians want to talk about the *Stone's* concert. They want us to help create a bit of chaos. Not sure if we want to be partners, but it doesn't hurt to listen. Does anyone here have tickets?"

Paul could only dream of the six dollars needed to get into the concert. What a show it would be.

"Nah, but Eddie and Frank do." Al lay on his back, hands behind his head.

"We'll have to sneak in to see the show. That's why I think we should listen to the Asians." Jim tossed his apple core to the ground and wiped his hands on his jeans.

The group nodded in agreement. Wouldn't hurt to listen. With the riots at *The Who* concert recently, the police would shut down any disturbances. If the Asians got tagged with the chaos, they might be able to sneak in for free.

Paul slipped into the plaid shirt; he belonged. The fabric comforted him, and he smoothed the bottom before nodding at Joe. It felt like a shield of armour. Nobody messed with the Clark Parkers.

CHAPTER TWELVE
February 26, 2018

He sat in the back. The shadow of the balcony above gave him a sense of security. People conversed in hushed whispers, but as expected, no one tried to include him in their conversations. CBC reporters sat a few rows forward and Global across the aisle. There were no cameras in the courtroom. He took great pains to avoid the cameras when he arrived. It would be more difficult to leave and not end up as some random in a newscast. Not that anybody'd likely notice him, but it was a loose end he didn't need. And he had come wearing a disguise, just in case.

They blew the bail hearing out of proportion on the news and this was no different. News stations were making a story out of nothing. They claimed the courts would disallow the DNA evidence. Then claimed the defendant's blood was planted at the scene of the murder.

While he liked what he was hearing, would the DNA evidence convict Paul Giovanni for a crime he didn't commit? That would be a disastrous outcome for both of them.

"All rise. The Honourable Judge Alisha Munroe presiding."

As he sat back down, he noted April Somersby lean over and whisper in Paul's ear. Paul nodded almost imperceptibly. What were they talking about?

He tuned out the judge's opening remarks and scanned the room. No one he recognized. Good. So far, they were letting him handle the situation. He had it in hand, and didn't need anyone else coming in and messing up his plans.

"Your Honour, the prosecution is making good progress in preparing the evidence for the murder of Lori Trembley on April 17, 1994."

A hush fell over the courtroom as the prosecutor rose and approached the judge. He presented the papers one by one.

"We can advise the Court that consistent with the charging document setting out the details of the murder of Lori Trembley, we have disclosed considerable evidence to the Defence, comprised of three witness statements from the time of the offence, including one statement identifying a man entering the apartment of Lori Trembley the day before the murder, matching Mr. Giovanni's description."

Paul's head dropped, but April continued to stare straight ahead.

"We have also disclosed forensic evidence related to fingerprints collected at the scene and a DNA expert's report accompanying the DNA evidence also gathered at the scene. In addition, we provided the Defence with the results of the blood test performed on Paul Giovanni, including the chain of custody documentation." The prosecutor paused in front of the judge.

The man at the back of the courtroom craned his neck, like everyone else in the courtroom, hoping he would glean information from the documents presented to the judge. A murmur rose from the gallery.

"Quiet." The judge raised her voice and glared at the gallery. "Have you disclosed all of your evidence to the Defence?"

"We have your Honour. We'll alert the court and the defence if any additional information comes to light."

"Ms. Somersby, do you have anything to add?"

"No, your Honour."

"In that case court is dismissed. We'll reconvene at a date to be set by the registrar to set a trial date."

The man at the back of the courtroom opened the door, hearing the judge's final words as it closed behind him. He pulled his cap low and hugged the shadows as he hurried to his car, where he waited for April Somersby to emerge and slide into her car two rows ahead. He needed to find out where she lived. Perhaps she kept some of her case materials at home. An easier target than the office.

A few minutes later, April Somersby emerged, threw her briefcase in the car, and turned into traffic. His Honda Civic followed at a distance. Her signal light indicated her turn onto the freeway. He followed with two cars between them. Ten minutes later she exited, and he followed until she pulled into her office parkade. He returned to the freeway and his penthouse suite. He'd have to be patient.

CHAPTER THIRTEEN
March 8, 2018

Paul walked the perimeter of the concrete yard. He used to walk with his head down, studying the cement, avoiding the gaze of others, but learned this was dangerous. He needed to remain alert to who was around him.

"Hey, Paul!"

Paul slowed, glancing over his shoulder as a guy fell into stride beside him, mumbling. "Keep walking."

Paul continued; hands shoved into his bomber pockets. He'd seen this guy around, but Paul kept to himself.

"Yeah?" Paul looked straight ahead, but in his periphery noticed the guy beside him glance to the right and left before speaking. "You're Paul Giovanni, aren't ya?"

"Yeah, who's asking?"

"You don't recognize me?" Paul glanced at him, squinted and tried to place him. "Sorry, man, but I'm terrible with names. You look vaguely familiar."

"Al, Al Jackman."

Paul's eyes widened. "Al, really. You're really Al Jackman?"

Al broke out in a grin. "The one and only. Been a few years."

Paul slowed, then shook his head and quickened his pace. "I've thought of you over the years and wondered what happened to you."

"Clearly not much good. Been waiting for trial for thirteen months."

"So, what're you charged with?"

Al glanced at Paul and lowered his voice to a barely audible whisper. "You don't ask a guy in here that question." He grinned and then chuckled. "What're you in for?"

Paul stared at the ground and shook his head. Al was as crazy as he remembered. He always was unpredictable. You never quite knew when he'd ignite. Paul learned early on you wanted to stay on Al's good side. It didn't matter if you were in the same gang. Al held you accountable and expected the same perfection he placed on himself. Paul didn't doubt that if Al focused his perfectionism on doing good for society, he could've been very successful.

"They got me on a cold case dating back to 1994. I didn't do it, but that doesn't seem to matter. Looks like they're keeping me in here till I prove my innocence. Guess I'm lucky. They've set trial for six months down the road."

A large man, Paul knew as Tiny, brushed past them. Suddenly, Al held his hand up between them and slowed to a stop. "Ah, okay, yeah, not sure I've heard about that case. Good luck with it." Al turned around and headed in the opposite direction.

Before he got too far, Paul turned and shouted after him. "Any other old Clark Parkers in here?"

Al batted the air like he was shooing a fly and kept walking in the direction they'd come.

Tiny slowed his pace and Paul caught up to him. The big guy was singing and his voice wasn't that bad. But when Paul heard the words, he stumbled.

"Ain't no mountain high enough, ain't no river wide enough, to keep me from getin' to you."

Tiny sang it repeatedly, getting louder each time. Finally, Paul spoke up. "Hey man, what's with the song? Those the only words you know?"

The singing stopped, and the air filled with tension. Tiny turned, a sneer dominating his face. "Just singin' it for you… Paul Giovanni." Then he burst into a maniacal laugh, sending shivers down Paul's spine.

Tiny was part of Paul's unit and they ended up in the yard together most days. He was big, no neck. At first, he thought maybe he was fat, but he soon came to realize the guy was solid, squat muscle.

Paul slowed down, and the singing started up again, although it faded as the distance between them increased.

In the dining hall that evening, Tiny lined up behind him. He felt the squat behemoth's eyes staring into his back. Paul shivered as Tiny's humming started up again.

Sweat broke out on Paul's forehead and he clutched his stomach with one hand and waved to get the guard's attention with the other. "Not feeling great. Can I go back to my cell?"

"Not a chance, sweet cheeks. If you're sick, you should've requested the infirmary. You'll have to make a request when you get back to your cell."

Paul fell into single file with the other ten inmates; Tiny was at his back as they loaded their plates.

When he turned at the end of the food line, Tiny dropped his plate. Paul wheeled around to see Tiny's grinning face. Paul's heart leapt into his throat. He dropped his plate and clenched his fists. This guy didn't appear to care what kind of reprimand he got. He was coming for him. The first punch hit his face, followed by one to the gut. Paul doubled over. But Tiny grabbed his hair and pulled him to within an inch of his face. "This is for Lori Tremblay, you sorry waste of space."

The next blow landed under his chin. Blackness surrounded him. *I didn't even get a punch in.* He heard whistles blowing, then the alarm. Then nothing.

*****

Paul woke the next day in the infirmary. He reached up to feel his face, but they'd tied his hands to the bed. He could barely see out of one eye and the other wouldn't open.

"Well, look who's come around."

The voice wasn't familiar. He craned his neck to see where it came from.

White walls and a white ceiling surrounded him. Other cots sat empty across from him. A tall, broad-shouldered man entered his periphery.

"I'm Ted, your nurse, for this delightful midnight to nine am shift. What can I get for you? Coffee, tea, croissants? Oh wait, we're fresh out of croissants. How about a piece of dry toast? I might be able to whip that up for you. You've been out for a while, likely starving." Ted left before Paul could tell him not to waste his time.

But then he smelled the bread toasting and his stomach growled. Maybe it would be okay after all.

Ted returned with toast and peanut butter, setting it on a table near the head of his bed. "Lucky you. I scrounged up a packet of peanut butter. Better than dry toast any day."

Paul mumbled a thank you, resulting in a series of coughs. His abdomen seared with pain.

"Okay, okay. Try to settle down. I'll raise the head of your bed, which should help. I'll do it slowly as I suspect your head isn't feeling too great right now.

Paul nodded, and another pain shot up the back of his neck, causing him to wince.

"Relax and let me do the heavy lifting."

Paul stared at Ted, standing at the foot of his bed. *Why are you being nice to me?*

"Okay, Paul, I'm going to untie your right wrist restraint. You won't try anything funny now, will you?"

Paul closed his eyes and shook his head. "I'm in no shape to try anything funny, Ted."

"Didn't think so."

Paul raised his hand and Ted placed the toast in it. He opened his mouth, his jaw ached, but he sank his teeth into the toast. Even his teeth hurt. He handed Ted the toast.

Ted leaned over and patted his shoulder. "There're no broken bones, just lots of bruising. You'll be feeling better soon. It's kind of late, but I can get you a phone call. Anyone you want to talk to?"

Paul thought about Nora. He didn't want her to worry. And if he called April, she'd likely tell Nora. "No, I think I'll keep quiet on this one. Can't see a phone call helping me out of this situation."

"Suit yourself, man, but next time, you might not be so lucky. If he'd wanted to kill you, though, he probably would have. I hope you got the message he was sending."

"Not a clue. He may have overheard me talking about my charges."

Ted raised his hands. "I stay out of the details. Just here to help you get better, and hope you don't return."

Paul closed his eyes while Ted tied his hand back to the bed.

*****

The next time he woke up, he felt much better. Tony who replaced Ted, wasn't nearly as caring.

"Looks like you're going home today. And by home, I mean that eight by ten cell you've earned."

Paul clenched his teeth. There was no sense professing his innocence and the whole injustice of the system. Tony would just tell him that's what everyone in here says. And he'd be right. No one admitted to their guilt.

Later that day, a guard accompanied him to his cell. He walked by Tiny's cell and his back muscles tensed. They had to know what had happened. It would all be on closed circuit footage. Tiny must be in solitary. He lay carefully on his bunk, closed his eyes, and tried to stop the pounding in his head. The guard's footsteps retreated down the hall.

"Psst, Paul. You, okay?"

Paul raised his head off the pillow and saw his cell mate leaning over the top bunk. "Yeah, I'll survive."

"Man, you had me worried. Thought you'd gotten yourself killed. The rumours spread that you were in the infirmary. How'd you get into this mess?"

Paul raised his head further. "Wish I knew. I was talking to a former old Clark Park gang member in the yard when this guy passed us. Then he turned on me."

"You're an old Clark Parker?"

"Yep. Been a long time, though."

"You realize Tiny's an old Riley Park gang member, right?"

Paul's eyes widened. It all made sense now. He hadn't counted on anyone from the old gang days.

After a long pause, Paul cleared his throat. "Do you think they'll move Tiny to another unit?"

"Hard to say. They try to separate guys not getting along, but if there's no room to move him, he may stay in the unit. I heard he got sent down to solitary, which won't sit well with him. He's not the type to give up on a vendetta. Watch your back, my friend."

CHAPTER FOURTEEN
March 10, 2018

Paul rolled over and faced the wall. His pillow didn't support his neck; fell flat, no matter how many times he fluffed it up. He closed his eyes to shut out his surroundings. But it was no use. Tiny stared back at him, anger in his eyes, spittle spraying as he spat out Lori Trembley's name.

His eyes snapped open, and he pulled his knees up to his chest. He wasn't counting on anyone connecting him to Lori. Hell, he'd worked hard all of his life to forget her. She influenced his life more now than when she was alive. He could only hope Tiny hadn't made the full connection.

But really, what did it matter? It wasn't like they'd ever haul Tiny into court to be a witness for the prosecution. Paul took a deep breath. The connection wasn't what he had to worry about, but staying alive until he made it to trial was.

The dinner bell rang and Paul stretched his legs and rolled over, bringing himself to his feet and making his way to the front of his cell. The door slipped open, and he stepped out. Al stared at him from across the hall. Talking wasn't allowed as they queued, but he could see the anguish in his eyes. Paul smiled, despite the pain, and shrugged his shoulders. Al hung his head and shook it slowly.

At the guard's orders, they fell into line, standing next to each other.

"Al I'm okay." Paul chanced a quick whisper. Al remained silent.

Once settled at their table with their plate of food, Paul continued his conversation. The clank of utensils on plates made it somewhat easy to have a private conversation. "Can you help me out? Are there other Riley Park members to watch out for?"

"Yeah, two others at the end of the table at the front of the room. One's bald, the other has long salt and pepper hair tied in a ponytail."

Paul tilted his water glass up and glanced to the front of the room. They faced his direction and stared straight at him. Paul lowered his head and continued to eat, regardless of the pain radiating from his jaw. "Shit, they're staring at me." His fork shook, and he set it down. "Jesus Christ, what am I going to do?"

"Word gets around quickly, so watch your back and avoid them at all costs. See if your lawyer can get you into one of the structured intervention units, but a fight that doesn't result in any serious injuries rarely warrants it."

"What's a structured intervention unit?"

"It's a fancy word for segregation. They don't call it segregation anymore, but it's the same thing. It's protection for those that need it. Full of pedophiles because we don't tolerate those psychos in the general population."

"Oh great, doesn't sound like a place I want to go."

"Yeah, wouldn't catch me there, but it might keep you alive."

Paul rolled the shrivelled peas around on his plate. He'd eaten all his jaw could manage.

Inmates filed past, and the two Riley Parkers strolled by the far end of Paul's table. They stared straight at him with wide grins. As they passed, Paul realized they were humming the same song Tiny had hummed the day he beat him up.

Paul grabbed his water glass and downed it. His breath came in short rasps and the glass shook as he set it down. At one time, he wouldn't have had any problem standing up for himself. Hell, he'd probably pick a fight, but it had been a long time since he'd acted that way. He ran a hand through his hair.

Al rose and walked away without even a glance in Paul's direction. Paul followed at a distance. No sense getting Al into trouble, too.

Paul shuffled back to his cell. He was exempt from the yard, so he laid on his bunk and thought about his situation. Surely, a beating like he received would be enough to request the intervention unit. Al couldn't be right about a fight not warranting it. Ted said he'd been lucky not to get killed. If Ted saw it like that, surely April could convince the warden to get him moved.

He closed his eyes and found himself face to face with two people from very different parts of his life, Tiny and Lori Trembley.

"Why'd you leave me like that, Paul?" Her voice was just as he remembered. Low and silky, with a rasp in just the right places. Her sorrow spoke to him through her eyes.

He wanted to tell her he panicked, but his voice wouldn't come out. His mouth opened and closed like a guppy. And Tiny stood behind Lori, his eyes bulging and red. Lori remained thirty-something and as beautiful as the last time he saw her.

Tiny stepped around Lori with a gun pointed at him. But as he pulled the trigger, Lori stepped in front and took the bullet. She smiled as she fell to the ground.

Paul woke with a start, sweat beaded at his hairline. Breath came in short rasps. He swung his legs over the bed and sat up.

"Guard! Guard!"

Boots echoed on the cement floor as they approached his cell. "What d'ya want?"

"I need to talk to my lawyer."

*****

Paul waited in the visitor's lounge. His right knee vibrated and his fingers tapped the table absently. What took her so long? She'd said she'd come right away. He glanced at the clock on the wall. It had been forty-five minutes since he'd called.

Finally, the door swung open and April strode in. She glanced around the room, eyes landing on Paul. Her face fell, and she rushed to the table. "What the hell? Who did this to you?" She reached out to touch his face, then pulled back. Either he was too disgusting to touch, or she realized even a gentle touch would hurt.

"It happened in the yard two days ago, and I got out of the infirmary today. Just bruises, they tell me, no broken bones."

"Two days ago? Why wasn't I contacted? They should have contacted me." April set down her notepad and pen, scribbling today's date at the top.

"I told them I didn't want to call anyone. I didn't want Nora to find out and worry."

"So, who did this to you?" April's eyes searched Paul's, desperate for an answer.

"It doesn't matter who did it. He's in a lockup. The important thing is, I want to get put in segregation or whatever they call it these days before he gets out. I don't think he's done with me yet."

April sat back in her chair, clearly fighting her emotions and trying to restore calm. After a long pause, she finally spoke up. "It does matter who it was and why he did it. If you want me to help you, you need to help me."

Paul inhaled deeply and shook his head. "Sorry, I don't know why he did it."

April raised her eyebrows, but remained silent.

"He was a member of the Riley Park gang. They were the Clark Park rivals back in the day. Apparently, he holds a grudge." Paul looked down at the table. It wasn't exactly the truth, but he hoped it would be enough for her.

"A grudge? That's some grudge. An almost fifty-year-old-grudge? What'd you do to make him beat you up now?" April squinted at him, cocking her head to the side.

"No idea, and I didn't have time to ask him. He's in my unit. I was talking to another former Clark Park gang member in the yard when, boom!" Paul pounded the table between them and April jumped again. "I passed out on the third blow, I believe. Clearly out of practice and a lightweight now. I didn't even get a counter punch in."

"Well, thank God for that. At least you won't have that against you when you go to trial. Now Paul, think back. What do you remember about this guy from the seventies? Did you fight him back then?"

"Honestly, April, I don't remember him at all. Hell, I barely recognized the other Clark Parker. But I've learned there are two others from the Riley Park gang with their eye on me, and I need to get out of the general population or I'm a dead man."

April slumped into her chair. "Listen Paul. As terrible as you look, and probably feel, one altercation is not enough to get you into the structured intervention units. They're usually very full and it's hard to get in. And besides, unless you want your gang relations brought up at your trial, I don't think we want to highlight this. I'm sorry. I know this sounds unjust."

"Come on April. There must be something you can do? I'm the walking dead in here." Paul sat forward, reaching out to

April without actually touching her.

She stared at his hands on the table. "If you think you're the walking dead, you better figure out why. Without a reason for this activity and the threat of more violence, my hands are tied."

Paul pushed away from the table. "Forget it. And don't tell Nora about this. I'll explain it to her myself the next time I see her."

"Paul, I'm sorry. You know I'd do something if I could."

"Like I said, forget it. Guard! Guard! I'm ready to go back.

Paul left the room without looking back. Al had warned him. He just didn't want to believe it was true.

CHAPTER FIFTEEN
March 17, 2018

"What's your favourite sport?" April sat across from David. This was their first official date. He'd made reservations at Ancora on the patio overlooking the water. The chill of the evening settled in, but her glass of wine warmed her inside. His foot brushed her calf. Was it an accident?

David rolled his eyes. "Hockey, of course. I even thought I'd be an NHL player one day."

"Were you that good?" April smiled at him. She liked him. Really, really liked him, and it had been a long time since she felt this comfortable with anyone.

David laughed. "Would I be a struggling financial broker if I could have played professional hockey?"

"Struggling my ass. Is a struggling financial broker a thing?"

"Oh, I assure you it is." He raised his glass to his lips, then continued. "You're right, however, I'm not struggling." He swallowed a mouthful of wine poured from the bottle he'd selected before she arrived.

April's phone buzzed, and she pulled it from her purse, glancing at the screen. "Sorry David, I have to take this."

He nodded and leaned back, staring out at the ocean.

"April Somersby."

"Hello Ms. Somersby. This is the warden at the Surrey Pretrial Services Centre. I'm afraid there's been an altercation involving your client, Mr. Giovanni."

April leaned forward. "What's happened?"

"During the hour in the yard, an inmate stabbed your client. He's in the prison hospital, undergoing surgery. I've been told it isn't serious, but you might want to alert his wife. He was coherent and insisted we call you and not her, but we don't feel comfortable if she's not notified."

April glanced up at David. So much for getting to know him better. "Okay, I'll be there in about half an hour."

She put the phone back in her purse. "I imagine you heard that."

David nodded and smiled. "I guess it's to be expected when you date the most wanted lawyer in Vancouver."

April blushed and glanced down. "Most wanted? I think not. But I have to go. My client's in surgery. Appears someone stabbed him during recreation time today." April stopped. She'd said too much.

"Oh no, well, of course you need to go. Are you okay to drive? Do you want me to take you?"

"I'm fine. Shaky, but I'm okay. Please stay and enjoy the view, the wine and have dinner. I'm glad I didn't order yet at least." April gathered up her purse and stood, pushing her chair in. She was also grateful she'd refused David's offer to pick her up and drive her to the restaurant. At least this didn't have to ruin his dinner.

David stood as well and reached for her arm, giving it a gentle squeeze. "We'll do this again, I promise. Now go. I hope your client's going to be alright."

She leaned in and gave him a peck on the cheek. "Thanks for being so understanding. I hoped we would get to know each other better tonight."

David smiled. "Well, I do like the sound of that."

April walked out of the restaurant, glancing back at David. He'd sat back down and had his phone out. *Hope he's not scrolling through Tinder.*

*****

When April arrived at the prison hospital, Paul was in recovery. The surgeon explained how the knife missed all vital organs. It was a wound to the gut, and that was never an easy recovery, but he was lucky.

April had called Nora. This altercation was more serious than last time. Nora rushed into the room just after the doctor delivered the post-op news. April held her by the shoulders. "Listen Nora, he's okay. The knife missed all organs, and he's going to be fine."

Nora collapsed into the chair beside her and sobbed. "Why, why? First, he was beat up and now this?"

April swallowed the lump in her throat. It was her fault. He'd requested the intervention unit, and she hadn't even asked. Was she just too lazy to do the paperwork? She stared at the floor. No. She did what she thought was best. Paul didn't need gang-related activities haunting him in court. He needed to look clean. But that notion was out the door. She'd demand intervention now, and she wouldn't be taking no for an answer.

"Nora, I'm sorry. This never should have happened. Paul told you about getting beat up a few days ago?"

Nora nodded, anger flashing in her eyes.

April raised her hand. "We didn't have a case before to get Paul segregated from the general population, but we do now. How much do you know about Paul's gang ties in the past?

Nora wiped her hand across her face and reached for a tissue on the table beside them. "I know quite a lot, but I'm sure I don't know everything. Paul's pretty ashamed of some of things he did as a teenager."

"Do you have any idea why someone from the old Riley Park gang would carry a grudge for almost fifty years?

Nora shook her head. "No, I can't imagine it. He's said the park gangs of the seventies weren't like they are now. They caused trouble in the neighbourhood and fought each other now and again. But they didn't use guns. No one ever killed anyone else. I mean, there was a cop who shot one of them, which helped to disband the Clark Parkers, but they were disbanding anyway. Most of the guys weren't interested in continuing down the path of gang member." Nora blew her nose and deposited the tissue in the garbage can on the other side of the room. "I'm sure some of them joined other gangs, but Paul turned his life around. He never seemed worried about his gang life coming back to haunt him."

April rose and patted Nora's back as they walked down the hall. "I guarantee I'll be making sure he's protected until the trial. There'll be hell to pay. How did an inmate get a knife, anyway? Someone's going to answer for this, and I won't quit till something's done."

Nora turned to April and hugged her. "Thank you."

April cleared her throat. Thanks, was the last thing she deserved.

CHAPTER SIXTEEN
March 19, 2018

He waited in the shadows of the underground parking lot where he had a view of April Somersby's car, a candy-apple-red Lexus. It stood out, and for that he was grateful. It was late, but he was determined to stay until she left the office this time.

He needed to come up with evidence soon. The Angels were getting restless. It was going to be tricky, but he needed to either break-in to her office or her home. The cameras and alarm system deterred him from the office. Maybe she'd take something home. He glanced at his watch. He prayed she hadn't decided to do an all-nighter at the office.

The parkade light flickered and went out. He smiled. *Couldn't have planned that any better.* A beam of light streamed out of the stairwell as the side door opened. April's silhouette, complete with briefcase, hesitated, reaching for her cellphone. Her phone flashlight glowed at the other end of the lot. Through his open window, he could hear the clip of her heels on the cement. She paused and shone her light toward him. He slumped lower in his seat and held his breath. Finally, her car door opened and her interior light glowed brightly. She hoisted what appeared to be a very heavy briefcase onto the passenger seat before settling in behind the wheel. Her engine roared to life, and she pulled out of the parking lot and up the ramp. Once she was out of sight, he started his engine and slowly made his way to the exit. Her left turn signal blinked in the distance. He sped to catch up.

There was enough traffic to keep him inconspicuous. His silver Honda civic, like him, didn't stand out. At last, the red sports car turned onto a side street. He slowed his car and parked, peering up the street. She pulled into a driveway, and a garage door opened. She entered, and the door closed behind her. He eased back onto the road and settled the Honda in the shadows of a Douglas Fir across from her house. The interior lights of her bungalow sprang to life. The venetian blind slats remained open, giving him a view of April pouring herself a glass of wine, then grabbing her briefcase and settling on the couch. She pulled out a folder and sipped her wine, flipping through papers. Suddenly, she leaned forward, placed her glass on the coffee table, and pulled two papers out, setting the folder beside her on the couch. She bent over, intently studying the pages, then suddenly sat up, a big grin on her face as she waved the papers in the air, like a victory celebration. She flipped the papers over, glancing at the backsides before placing them in her lap and leaning back after reaching for the wineglass. After a few minutes she returned the papers to the folder and the folder to her briefcase. She rinsed the glass in the sink, leaving the briefcase on the couch, and turned off the light. A light at the far end of the house went out twenty minutes later.

He glanced at his watch. Ten past twelve. He'd give her till one and hope she fell asleep quickly after a long day. He leaned back in his seat, about to close his eyes, when he noticed movement on the sidewalk in his rear-view mirror. Someone walked toward his car. He slunk down below the headrest, sitting still so as not to garner attention.

"Come on Max, let's go."

He glanced in the mirror, but the person was no longer in his sight-line. Then he was there. Standing beside his car. If the passenger door opened, it would have hit him. He breathed shallowly, aware of the passenger window open a crack. The person picked up something, then the jingle of dog tags receded as he turned and walked back the way he came.

The man exhaled and rested his neck on the head rest before closing his eyes. The next time he opened them, it was twenty past one. He grabbed his small toolkit and exited his vehicle, closing the car door softly. He scanned the neighbourhood. No motion, no lights. Everyone was sound asleep, as they should be. He shone his pen light on the door, and then rifled through his tools, finding the one to work best on the lock. Within seconds, the door opened, and he slipped inside. He closed the door soundlessly and froze. No sound. He shone his penlight on the couch and found the briefcase right where April left it. She hadn't zipped it up, and the folder stuck out about an inch. He reached in and pulled it out. The first two pages were face down. They must have been the pages she took an interest in before retiring for the night. He turned them over, shone his pen light on them and snapped photos before replacing them. A floorboard creaked in the hallway. He crouched down instinctively and waited. Soon, April rounded the corner and headed straight for the kitchen. He glanced at the front door. His eyes had adjusted to the dim interior and he could see he hadn't re-locked it. Hopefully, she wouldn't notice.

A cupboard door opened and closed. Water ran from the faucet, then all was quiet. She reappeared, turned the corner and shuffled down the hall. He waited a few minutes, then slipped out the door. He settled into his car; his breathing heavy. Again, he waited, not wanting to start the engine and give April a reason to look outside. He felt his heart beating in his temples. He was getting soft. How many times had he done this type of thing? Was he was getting too old for this?

Back at his place, he sent the pictures to his computer and printed them out. His eyes widened. She had evidence that might find Paul not guilty. A smile spread across his face, and he breathed a sigh of relief.

He poured himself a drink and sat on the balcony listening to the buses roar by below. "To DNA evidence." He raised his whisky and clinked an imaginary glass in front of him. "May it tell enough truth to get Paul off and me out of hot water."

CHAPTER SEVENTEEN
June 3, 1972

Paul stood outside the Pacific Coliseum, where hundreds had assembled for the Rolling Stones concert. He gazed up at the building. *June 3, 1972, will be the best night of my life.* Stevie Wonder belted out lyrics to a backdrop of hoots and cheers as the crowd inside awaited the headline act. Paul waited for the cue to storm the side door.

Eddie and Frank were already inside with legitimate tickets. The Asian gang members loitered nearby. Electricity filled the air with anticipation of an uprising. They wanted to improve on the riot at the last Stone's concert; put Vancouver on the map with the Asian gang dead centre. The Clark Parkers hadn't said they wouldn't take part, but they had no intention. They'd be part of the crowd when the chaos broke out, then slip in through a side door and enjoy the party.

Somebody in the crowd threw a rock and then the police were in front of them in full riot gear. Jim grabbed Paul's sleeve and pulled him forward, inching closer to the side door. The riot gear incited the crowd to yell and throw whatever they could get their hands on. Al, ahead of them, reached the door and pulled. It didn't budge. He banged on it, but no one opened it from the other side. The crowd pushed; the police pushed back. Then the batons came out. Paul's eyes widened, and he looked at Jim for guidance. He couldn't hear what he said, but he could read his lips. *RUN!*

Jim let go of his sleeve and before long, Paul lost sight of him. He tripped over something, catching himself before he hit the pavement. When he looked down, Al laid at his feet curled up in a ball as people walked over him. Paul grabbed his hand, pushing people off and creating a barrier until Al found his footing. Then they were both off.

Al wove through the crowd like a pro. Paul had never been in a mob before. The crowd pushed him back toward the police line and his fellow Clark Parkers were nowhere to be seen. He fought against the wave, but it was one step forward, two steps back, and soon he came face-to-face with a shield and a baton. He dropped to his knees, instinctively throwing his hands in the air.

The other Clark Parkers talked about their arrests like badges of honour, but Paul didn't see the honour in it. His mother's disappointed face flashed through his mind. She didn't deserve this. She didn't know he was part of a gang, going against her wishes. Bile rose in his mouth. He kept his gaze down.

Cuffs snapped onto his wrists, and he was lifted and dragged behind the line of cops to a paddy wagon. He sat inside, studying the faces surrounding him. Some were smug, some terrified, like him. Would he go to Juvie? He'd heard Al refer to Juvie as a vacation home. A place to make friends, form alliances, and learn about new ways to commit crimes.

Although it occurred to Paul, if those guys knew how to commit crimes, they wouldn't be in Juvie.

A couple more guys stumbled into the wagon before the doors closed, and it inched its way out of the stadium grounds toward the downtown station.

The cuffs bit into Paul's wrists. He tried to relax, but his heart pounded in his chest, and his tongue stuck to the roof of his mouth. At least twenty people sucked the oxygen out of that wagon. He concentrated on his breathing, trying to shut out the surrounding noise. As he breathed in, the stench of sweat and blood and stale cigarette smoke clinging to clothes choked him. He needed air. He glanced around, his breath coming in brief gasps. There were no windows. No way to get air. He bowed his head and closed his eyes. He envisioned his mother hugging him. It was the most comforting thing he could think of.

The brakes squealed, and the wagon lurched to a stop. The other boys stomped their feet and rocked back and forth, causing bile to rise once again into the back of Paul's throat.

Then the doors flew open, fresh air rushing into the vacuum created by too many people in too small of a space. Paul gulped the air like he was drinking a coke. It caught in the back of his throat and he coughed as much as he inhaled. He was the first to get out. He didn't care what it was like in jail. It couldn't be worse.

"Okay, you bunch of shitheads, follow Officer McCann. He'll show you where your sleeping quarters are."

But Officer McCann didn't deliver as promised. He opened the door to the station. Chaos ensued inside, and McCann came to an abrupt halt. Paul, who was right behind him, ran into him. With his hands tied behind his back, he fell to his knees. Officer McCann turned with his baton raised above his head, then looked down and saw Paul on his knees, staring up with pleading eyes.

"Sorry Officer, I didn't mean to. Didn't know you were stopping." Paul ducked his head, anticipating where the baton would land.

"That's the politest thing any of you hoodlums have said to me tonight." He leaned down and pulled Paul to his feet. He leaned over and whispered. "As you can see, this place is overfull. I'm going to lean over and undo your cuffs if you promise to ease your way out of here slowly, and promise me I'll never see your sorry ass again."

Paul nodded. "Promise, sir." He sidestepped the door after the cuffs fell off. He kept to the side streets, avoiding the many patrol cars as they headed back to the Stone's concert.

Paul glanced at the clock as he slipped in the front door, the silence of emptiness deafening. His dad was out, and his mom wasn't yet home from work. He lay on the couch, pulling the blanket slung over the back on top of him. Minutes later, the door opened and his mother groaned as she pulled off her shoes. Paul peered out from under the blanket.

"Hello Ma. You, okay?"

He heard the smile in her voice. "Just fine, son. So glad you're home. The streets out there are crazy tonight."

Paul closed his eyes and said a quick prayer. He didn't ask for forgiveness for what he'd done, but rather for keeping his dark secret from his mother for at least one more day.

CHAPTER EIGHTEEN
March 20, 2018

April gazed out her picture window. Rays of sun sifted through the lifting fog. The bark of the old cedar rugged against the grey haze. The builder had tried to convince her to remove the tree, but it was the reason she chose this property. She was thankful she'd stuck to her principles.

The coffee warmed her hands, and she blew on it absently. Another sleepless night, or at least it seemed sleepless. Her Fitbit claimed she had five hours, twenty-two minutes. It showed her in a deep sleep, then wide-awake half an hour later. It was the way most nights went lately. A glass of water made her have to get up three times.

She flipped through the evidence one more time. No gun recovered, no fingerprints, the only thing the prosecution had was DNA. She studied the two pages she'd focused on the night before. Hair. There were several strands of hair at the scene. When the prosecution ran the DNA, neither Paul nor the victim were matches, not even partial matches. The prosecution failed to highlight this interesting tidbit during discovery. Just lumped it in with DNA evidence, hoping she wouldn't look at all the pages closely.

Hairs could be left lying around at any time, but in this case, they found hairs in the victim's right hand with the root-ball attached to most of them, suggesting Lori Trembley pulled them out of the head of her attacker. It was all in the file.

April leaned back on the couch and sipped her coffee. Most people liked their coffee steaming hot, but she wasn't like most. She preferred it lukewarm. And she only needed one cup to get her going. The odd time she'd have another in the early afternoon, and today would be one of those days. She closed her eyes and rested her head against the top of the couch. *Why are mornings more preferable to sleep than evenings?*

Thoughts of David floated in, and she smiled. If only they could have finished their date the other night. A tingle crawled up her spine, anticipating the next time they'd get together. As if on cue, her cell phone vibrated. She picked it up off the couch and glanced at it.

Hope your client's okay. The bottle of wine was lovely, but I don't want to rub it in. Had to take a cab home, though. Any chance you have time for dinner tonight? Probably too late to get reservations at that restaurant, but I can choose another? And I can pick you up. Let me be your designated driver.

Right now, her days were not hers. She couldn't predict if she'd be able to meet him or not. She stared at the front door. When did she last use the front door? She always went through the garage.

That's when she noticed the deadbolt. Straight up and down. Vertical. Not in the locked position. How long had it been that way? It always remained locked. The saliva drained from her mouth and she shivered. When had she unlocked her front door? She racked her brain trying to remember the last time she entered or exited through that door. She hadn't been home during the day for ages. When was the last time she opened it? Her mind drew a blank. It had to have been months. She would have noticed an unlocked door before now. Wouldn't she?

She opened the door and peered out into the front yard like the answer to her question would magically appear, then closed it, turned the deadbolt, and leaned against it. She exhaled and thanked the powers that be for keeping her safe. Her eyes snapped open, and she scanned the room. Her purse sat on the kitchen island where she'd left it the night before. She opened the cabinet near the front door. It was a mess, but her spare set of car keys sat on top of the heap. Nothing appeared to be disturbed. She shook her head and stumbled into the kitchen, dumping the rest of her coffee down the drain and rinsing out the cup before leaving it inverted in the sink.

She grabbed her phone and texted David back.

Tonight, sounds great, but I can't commit to dinner. Let me see how my day unfolds. Maybe meet for a drink somewhere if my day goes sideways?

A thumbs-up emoji appeared on her phone before she stepped into the shower to wash away the remnants of a restless night.

*****

April stopped by the hospital before going into the office. She wanted to share the hair evidence with Paul; no doubt he could use the good news. She also had an appointment with the warden to discuss the plan for Paul's return to the prison. He damn well better have a spot for him in structured intervention. For people like Paul, it was necessary.

After signing in, April stood at Paul's door. Nora sat by his bedside. Both slept. She paused, then turned around. Her news could wait. She left the hospital and drove straight to the warden's office. Her appointment wasn't for another hour, but maybe she'd get in early.

She tapped her foot. The administrative assistant peered over her glasses and shook her head. April stilled her foot. She'd handed her phone in at the front, so she couldn't even check messages as she waited.

Finally, the warden stuck his head out and called her in.

"Ms. Somersby, let's just get right to the point. I saw your request for a structured intervention unit for Paul Giovanni. It isn't necessary. The man who stabbed him is in lock-up, and we'll be moving him so they'll no longer be in the yard together."

"Now Warden. You know as well as I do that shuffling the chairs on the Titanic is not the answer. This is gang related. Remove one man and another will replace him. My client isn't safe, and there's no way to predict who will threaten him next. If there's ever a case for structured intervention, this is it. And you know it." April stared into his eyes, unwavering. If he expected her to cave, he was sorely mistaken.

"And Ms. Somersby, I'm sure you know we're bursting at the seams in structured intervention. I have no room." The warden's scowl would deter most people from arguing.

"That should tell you something, Warden. Why're your units full? Does it mean the population of inmates under your control is out of control?" April leaned forward, placing her hands on the edge of his desk.

"It's the same everywhere. We don't have a unique problem here."

"Well, that's interesting. The media would love to dive in and bring this problem to light, especially if they have a personal story to highlight." April sat back and folded her arms across her chest. She would not be brow beaten by this patriarchal misogynist.

The warden paused, his gaze lowered to the desk, and he cleared his throat. He pulled a paper from the bottom of the pile in front of him. "Okay, Ms. Somersby. I'll see what I can do. I'll draw up a plan for his return by the end of the day." He rose and glanced at the door. April's cue to leave.

"Thank you, Warden." She turned and let herself out. *Bastard.* He thought he could roll right over her. Why did she always have to prove herself and fight the old-boys' network? She glanced at her watch. Ten o'clock. She pulled her car back onto the freeway and drove to the hospital.

*****

Paul raised his head by pressing the button on the side of his bed. He tried to scoot up, but the pain from his side seared across his abdomen. He let out a grunt. "Shit!" he collapsed back against the pillow and closed his eyes, waiting for the pain to subside.

"Here, Paul, you can have another Tylenol."

Paul opened his eyes and took the tiny paper cup from the nurse. "Morphine's what I need, not a damn Tylenol." But he knew former drug users weren't offered the good stuff.

"Try to lie still and let yourself heal."

His intravenous pole beeped, and he rolled his head to the side. The nurse opened the front of the IV dispenser, flicked the bubbles, and reset the alarm.

Paul closed his eyes and took a few shallow breaths.

"No, no, he's not asleep."

Paul opened his eyes as the nurse exited the room and April walked in.

She stared at the floor, glancing up at him. "Hey Paul. I was in earlier, but you and Nora were sleeping, so I didn't want to disturb you." She sat on the chair beside the bed.

"Yeah, I sent her home. We didn't get much sleep last night."

"I'm so sorry this happened. I can't tell you how sorry I am for not pushing for segregation."

Paul remained silent.

"Well, I won't keep you long. I have a couple of pieces of good news that I hope might brighten your day."

Paul's eyes searched hers. "Forgive me if I don't jump up and down."

April sighed. "The warden is putting together a plan for your return. He's getting you into one of the structured intervention units to protect you from the general population."

Paul exhaled. "Thanks, I appreciate that."

"Just part of my job. Sorry it took a stabbing to make it happen. The system's broken."

"Yeah, broken. So broken, they stabbed an innocent man wrongly incarcerated. I'm not sure how much I can take."

"Don't give up. My second bit of good news is I've found a crack in the case. I reviewed the folder of evidence last night and found two pages outlining the DNA results of several hairs found at the scene. Their DNA profiles don't match yours or Lori Trembley's."

Paul closed his eyes and exhaled. "Don't think that's worth much. Wouldn't there be unmatched hairs at most crime scenes?"

"Yes, there would be, but these had intact root-balls, and they found most of them in the victim's right hand. That's significant. It's logical to assume she pulled hair from the head of the guy attacking her."

Paul opened his eyes and stared at the ceiling. "Well, that's something, I guess. Thanks April."

"Paul, it is something. You should be more excited about this. Things are looking up."

Paul smiled weakly but didn't respond. Hope seemed elusive. A few hairs? Not much to go on. How could they hinge his entire case on that?

April rose and stared out the window before turning back to Paul. "Well, I'll let you get some rest."

Paul nodded. "Thanks." After watching her exit the room, he turned his attention to the ceiling. He was being hard on her, and he felt badly for it. She brought good news. He wouldn't have to worry about Tiny and his friends any longer, and maybe the hair would help create doubt about his guilt. It didn't erase him from the scene, but it proved someone else was there. Maybe he'd have to tell April what else happened that day. He had to think about it.

CHAPTER NINETEEN
March 20, 2018

One eye opened as he slid his phone off the nightstand. Ten forty-three. He sat up and swung his legs over the side of the bed. The events of the night before came into focus as he stood over the toilet. Maybe he'd get to fly out of this God-forsaken city tonight. He brushed his teeth and hair, wetting down the sides. He studied his reflection. It would pass. Needed a cup of coffee, though. He snapped his watch on his wrist. Seven minutes. He pulled on a polo shirt and jeans and headed to the kitchen, thankful for the Nespresso machine. Positioning himself on the bar stool, he put his phone on the counter and took a long draw on his coffee. He closed his eyes, relaxed, and focused on returning home.

The phone rang and brought him back to reality. A gruff face filled the screen.

"Anything to report?"

He inhaled before responding. "Actually, yes. I trailed April

Somersby home late last night, then broke into her house, and found some very interesting evidence that the prosecution hadn't yet reported."

He waited for a response, but when there wasn't one, he continued. "It looks like there was hair found at the scene. I mean several strands with root-balls attached. And their DNA doesn't belong to Lori Trembley or Paul Giovanni, and they found the hair in Lori's right hand."

"That doesn't explain the blood at the scene, though, does it?"

"No, but doesn't that prove I was there? I can't help it if someone else dripped their blood on my crime scene." He cleared his throat, even he heard the whine in his voice.

"You were paid for that hit. And your track record hasn't always been squeaky clean. Your client has questioned your actions in the past. But this time you've really pushed the limits of their trust. Your reputation's tarnished. You'll never get another job in this industry if Paul Giovanni goes down for this. Trust is hard to earn back."

"I know, I know. But I don't want them to tag me for it. Isn't my hair at the scene enough to prove I was there? I did the job."

"Your hair? That's presumptuous, isn't it? I pulled the file. You said you bled on the scene before leaving. How could that blood be someone else's? You've proven nothing. The only way you're off the hook is if they acquit Paul Giovanni. A few hairs at the scene of the crime aren't enough to do that."

He controlled his face. Video could amplify even the

slightest move or emotion, and he didn't want to give this man the slightest sign of his disappointment. This foray into his past cost him money. Big money. But more than that, it could end his career.

"I swear I did the job. It was a long time ago and definitely the sloppiest job I ever did. But I'll never forget the look on Lori Trembley's face as I pointed the gun at her. You can bet I did the job, and I did it alone." The man swallowed and stared straight at the camera.

"Well better find something else a bit more substantial. You may need a hail Mary to get out of this one. From what I've read, the prosecution has a pretty solid case. It doesn't look good for you."

The screen went black. No hello, no goodbye. Just there one minute, gone the next. He threw the phone across the room where it hit the wall and bounced back. He ran a hand across the back of his neck. Looked like rainy Vancouver would be home for a while yet.

He slowly rose and bent over to pick up his phone. Screen intact, no worse for wear. Those Otter Boxes were amazing. Where was April Somersby this morning? Did she notice her unlocked front door? He smiled. He enjoyed messing with people's minds.

Patience. At least the defence appeared to be competent. If Paul had a public defender, it would be lights out for him and Paul. He stripped, hanging his shirt and jeans in the closet. He'd never had a serious relationship. There was no room for that in his line of work. But the odd one-night stand turned into a week or two. They always commented on his perfectionism. By the time he left them, he'd had enough of their chaos. He liked his solitary lifestyle. No mess. No ties. And lots of money. Although often on the job, he had to play that down. Like the Honda Civic. It irked him to no end that he had to drive around Vancouver in something so mundane. But this job called for mundane, he understood that.

He pulled out his workout gear and headed to the on-site gym. Maybe he'd find someone there to take his mind off this rainy shithole.

As he pounded out the miles on the treadmill, he realized what his next step needed to be. It was risky, but what was reward without risk? He smiled to himself. Risk was what he needed to get his blood pumping again.

CHAPTER TWENTY
March 23, 2018

Paul lay on his cot, staring into space. He did that a lot since returning from the hospital. Segregated from the general population allowed him to breathe easier, but it was lonely. Nora's visits also became less frequent, but maybe it was for the best. He hated her seeing him this way.

Stan rapped on his door. "Someone to see you." He studied a paper in his hand. "A Sam White?"

Paul liked Stan. In fact, all the guards treated him well. Probably easier to be nice to a guy accused of murder than a pedophile. Somehow, he was at the top of the heap on this side. He cocked his head. "Who did you say was here?"

"Sam White. Says he's a friend of a friend. Should I tell him to go away?"

Paul grinned. "Are you kidding? I don't have enough friends to turn one away. Besides, it'll kill a bit of time."

Paul stood at the front of his cell, hands outstretched, head down. He followed Stan down the hall to the visitation centre and sat at a table at the back. He'd learned to keep his back to the wall in this place. Last thing he needed was to fall into complacency and end up dead. He watched the door at the front, waiting for it to open. *Sam White?* Didn't ring a bell at all. But if he was a friend of a friend, it wouldn't. Maybe he had some tidbit of information for him. Something to help him out.

The door opened and a tall man, middle-aged, waited as a guard pointed in Paul's direction. But Paul noted his eyes fell on him long before the guard directed him. Clearly, Sam recognized him, but that wasn't a surprise either. The media had plastered his face all over the news for months.

He held his hands under the table as the man approached. He extended his hand toward Paul, but Paul raised his hands, showing him the cuffs.

"Oh, of course. Sorry about that." Sam settled into the seat across from him.

Paul stared back, trying to place him. Something about him looked familiar, but he drew a blank.

"You're clearly wondering who I am?"

Paul nodded and cocked his head, focused on the guy's eyes. Was there something familiar about them?

Sam averted his gaze and stared at the tabletop. "Someone you know sent me. A guy named George. George Russo."

Paul inhaled sharply. He remembered George, a former Clark Parker he tried to avoid back in the day. He'd watched him beat up people with no regard for who they were; kids, old ladies, didn't matter to him. Paul didn't want to be associated with him. He saw his mugshot on TV in the mid-nineties. They claimed he'd migrated to the Angels, and he was caught dealing drugs. Paul couldn't remember what his sentence came to, but it felt like it was a good chunk of time. The guy sitting across from him didn't look like he'd hang out with George.

"Really. How do you know George?"

Sam leaned forward, keeping his voice low. "The way most people know George. A work acquaintance."

Paul stared into Sam's face, pausing before he continued. "So, why're you here, Sam?"

"George wanted me to offer you, our services. Thought we might help you out. Not sure your lawyer, uh, what's her name? April…"

"Somersby."

"Yeah, that's it, Somersby. Not sure she's doing you any good. We have much deeper and further reaching connections."

Paul raised his hand. He ran his tongue over the back of his teeth. "I'm quite happy with my legal counsel, thanks." He swung his legs to the side.

"Wait, Paul, hear me out."

Paul sat back against his chair. Wouldn't hurt to hear what he had to say. "Okay, I'm all ears."

"Look, we have people in high places." Sam glanced around before continuing. "What do they have on you? Maybe we can make the evidence disappear."

Paul chuckled. "You're a piece of work." Paul sobered up quickly when he realized it wasn't the best idea to piss this guy off, and in turn, George. "I mean that in the best way possible." He cleared his throat and started again. "Look, the prosecution has divulged the evidence, and there's no going back now. They've set the wheels in motion. Like the news is saying, they've got my blood at the scene."

"But you didn't do it, did you, Paul? I mean, you may have contributed to Lori's death, but you didn't put the bullet in her, did you?"

Paul's heart pounded in his chest. What did this guy know, and how? He ran a tongue over his lips. How could Sam possibly know about that day? Did he know who shot Lori Trembley? He shook his head.

"No, sure didn't. I'm not sure why you think I contributed to Lori's death. I'm innocent." Paul glanced up at the guard stationed at the door. "Listen Sam. I'd love to stay and chat, but I've got a book to read. Tell George I appreciate the thought, but I'm good. I've been out of gangs for almost fifty years, and I want to remain that way."

Sam exhaled and shook his head. "Big mistake, man. Our lawyers could work for you, pro bono. Won't cost you a thing."

Paul forced a grin and rose from the table. He saw a glint in Sam's eyes he was sure he'd seen before. Had he come here to offer him lawyer services on behalf of the gang, or did he have another motive? His legs buckled, but he straightened and strode toward Stan. Paul didn't look back. He shivered and allowed Stan to guide him back to his cell.

*****

April sat in the warden's office. She took a deep breath. He stared at her, a slight grin on his face.

"What can we do for you today?" His tone was laced with sarcasm.

She cleared her throat, her knuckles white as she clasped her hands in her lap. "You can tell me why someone visited my client yesterday. He's segregated. Not supposed to have unapproved visitors. What the hell's going on in your jail, Warden?"

He leaned back in his chair and put his right foot on his knee, his hands behind his head. "I don't know what you're talking about, Ms. Somersby."

"Well, you better find out. They offered my client a different lawyer's services. Is it common practice for you to allow people to visit segregated inmates and have them slander their counsel?" April stopped before she said more. Her face burned; her pulse reverberated in her ears.

The warden leaned forward. "I told you. No one visited your client. Mr. Giovanni is making stuff up now. I've checked the logs. No one signed in or out to see your client yesterday. Maybe he's just trying to tell you he's firing you." A grin returned to his face, and he rocked back and forth in his office chair.

April's eyes narrowed. "It better not happen again. You hear me? The press is going to hear about this if something happens to my client." As she left the room, slamming the door behind her.

Her anger hadn't dissipated when she reached the parking lot. Sitting behind the wheel tears stung her eyes. They wouldn't see her tears of frustration. She swore after the stabbing she'd keep Paul safe. And she thought she had. Now this.

She dialed David's number, and he picked up on the second ring.

"Hey beautiful. I love it when you call me in the middle of the day."

April burst into sobs.

"Hey, hey, hey. What's happened? You, okay?"

She could hear the concern in his voice. While their relationship hadn't progressed beyond the odd dinner or drink, she wished it had. But she'd been distant, trying to concentrate on the case, and her roster of other cases that seemed to pile up.

She took a deep breath. He waited for her reply.

"I'm fine. Just frustrated, that's all. Needed to hear a friendly voice."

"Okay, you can't just say that. Tell me. What's happened?"

April let it all out. Told David about the warden and his misogynistic attitude. About Paul's visitor and the warden's denial. About her fears of something happening to Paul before the trial. "Are you there, David?"

"Oh sure, yeah. I was giving you space. Wasn't sure you were done. I'm sorry that's happening to you, April. Do you want to meet? Sounds like you could use a shoulder to lean on. I'm a pretty good listener."

April sighed. Why was she holding off getting closer to this guy? Because he was too perfect? What did that say about her? Didn't she deserve a good man?

"Oh David. I've already said too much. I have meetings this afternoon that I can't blow off. Thanks for picking up and letting me vent. I'll be okay. But I think I need to call off our meet-up tonight. Sorry, but I just need some alone time."

"Okay, but if you change your mind, I'm here for you."

CHAPTER TWENTY-ONE
November 28, 1972

Paul closed his eyes and concentrated on his breathing. His lungs burned, and he wanted to take a gulp of air, but didn't dare.

They'd scattered when Ian threw the car into park. Tires screeched above the police sirens, then the door flung open and shouts of 'freeze, police' cut through the noise. But he didn't freeze. He ran into the shadows, glimpsing Joe up ahead, running to what Paul knew was a wall. Joe was limber, though. He'd be able to scale it. Paul veered to the left, down an alley lined with garbage bins. He tried a few back doors of businesses, all locked. Fire consumed his lungs, and he ducked behind a large bin, holding his breath and listening. No footsteps coming after him, but the shouting in the distance was unmistakable. A shot rang out, maybe two? Or maybe an echo? Paul controlled his exhale, then sucked air in quietly. He heard frantic voices, more sirens, but couldn't make out what anyone said.

A shot. It must have been from a cop, since none of the Clark Parkers had guns. His hands shook and sweat stung his eyes. He wiped a sleeve across his face and peeked out. No sign of movement.

He slipped out of his plaid shirt and stuffed it into the bin, straightened his T-shirt, and strolled out of the enclave into the alley. Keeping to the shadows and forcing himself to walk, not run. When he reached the main street, he headed north. A few more blocks and he'd be home.

Police cars sped by, none taking notice of a fourteen-year-old in a black T-shirt, hands stuffed in his jeans' pockets. He opened the main door of their apartment's five floor walk-up. It was quiet. Too quiet. No neighbours or his parents fighting, no TVs blaring. Calm with a tension that raised the hair on Paul's arms. He turned the doorknob. Locked. They never locked the door. They had nothing worth stealing. He knocked, hoping his dad was passed out and his mom would hear him. Silence greeted him from the other side. He slumped to the floor when the door across the hall opened a crack. Mrs. Ricci peered out, then opened her door wider.

"Paul, what are you doing sitting in the hall?" Mrs. Ricci stood in front of Paul in a blue floral house dress, hair in curlers, a cigarette hanging from her mouth.

He nodded his head toward the door handle. "Locked."

"Aren't your parents home? I swear I heard them about an hour ago. Your poor mother works so hard, then comes home to him." Mrs. Ricci's hand flew to her mouth. "Sorry, I shouldn't have said that."

Paul dismissed her apology with a wave of his hand. "No worries Mrs. Ricci. I feel the same way." Then he rose to his feet. "Hey do you have a wire? I'm sure I can jimmy the lock open."

Mrs. Ricci held up her index finger before disappearing inside her apartment and quickly returning with a bobby pin, holding it up with skepticism.

"Perfect!" Paul grabbed the bobby pin, bending it open, and inserting it into the lock. The door handle turned. He held out the bobby pin to Mrs. Ricci, who looked at it with disdain, and Paul realized it wasn't much good for holding hair in place any longer. "Oh, sorry."

Mrs. Ricci smiled. "That's okay, Love, I've got lots. Maybe keep that in your pocket for future needs. Now go get some sleep. A boy your age shouldn't be out wandering the streets at this hour." Her words rambled through her door as she closed it, and the lock clicked into place.

The second he entered the apartment, he smelled it; the sweet metallic aroma of blood, mixed with stale beer and cigarette smoke. His throat closed, and he fell to his knees. When his eyes adjusted to the light, his entire body shook. He crawled across the floor to his mother's body through a pool of sticky liquid and laid his head on his mother's motionless chest. An anguished cry escaped his trembling lips. He listened for signs of his father, before rising and grabbing a knife off the kitchen counter. The street lights flooded the apartment, and bloody footprints led to the bedroom. He kicked open the door. His father lay motionless on the bed. Paul raised the knife, then noticed the blood-soaked blanket, his father's open eyes, and the ghastly wound across his neck. The knife used to slice the Christmas turkey resting in the palm of his outstretched hand.

Paul doubled over and vomited on the floor beside the bed.

He stumbled back into the kitchen and picked up the phone.

*****

Paul rocked back and forth; eyes closed. The smell of fresh blood soured as he sat. How long would it take the police to arrive? It took everything in his being not to run. But his mom deserved more. She deserved his respect. He'd stay for her. He rose and cracked open a window. The cool November air wafted in and he pressed his nose against the screen, gulping in every molecule. At last, a police cruiser pulled up below. Lights flashing, but no siren. Two officers emerged and strolled toward the front entrance. Paul walked past his mother to the door and opened it.

He remembered little about what happened next, but the lonely feeling of being without his mother was something he'd never forget. The officers' voices were distant, and he stood on a path alone. He tried to listen to what they were saying, but their voices echoed from far away. For the first time in his life, it felt comforting to be in the backseat of a police cruiser. He rocked back and forth, his knees vibrating.

That was the day Paul became an ex-Clark Parker. It was the day he entered the foster care system and the day that set him on the path to finding Nora.

CHAPTER TWENTY-TWO
April 12, 2018

"How does the defendant plead?"

The judge's words echoed in a silent but overcrowded courtroom. The man sitting at the back of the room held his breath as his mind wandered back to April 17, 1994.

His first contract and things went sideways. But he learned from his mistakes, forever wary of glass coffee tables. He pulled the trigger in haste, all his plans gone by the wayside. There was so much blood he couldn't tell which was hers and which was his. Then sirens pierced the night air, and he left in a hurry, changing into a fresh set of clothes after wrapping his injuries, and catching the first plane to Los Angeles.

The horror in her eyes never left him. He could recall her face as if he'd seen her minutes before. His victims since then were faceless. Just jobs. For a few reasons, she was different. She was a regret. And he was having to relive it all over again. Under any other circumstances, he'd love to find someone else to take the blame, but he needed credit for the work he'd done and couldn't allow someone else to take the fall. And besides, deep down, he had to admit he felt a debt of gratitude to Paul.

Gangs demanded accountability. After this many years, you'd think they could let it go, but it wasn't to be.

He shook his head and refocused on the front of the courtroom.

Paul Giovanni cleared his throat and straightened his shoulders. "I plead not guilty."

No surprise there. The poor sod wasn't guilty.

The judge continued on in her monotonous tone, instructing the parties involved of their duties.

The man's head rose as April Somersby stood. "Your Honour, we would like to waive our right to a preliminary inquiry and request an early date for trial be expedited. My client has suffered not just one attack in jail, but two. The second was a stabbing. The court doesn't want the blood of an innocent man on its hands. We request a trial to be expedited for the safety of my client."

The man could have sworn the judge rolled her eyes. How many times did they hear that request from a defendant?

"Ms. Somersby. The court docket is full. It's not possible to move your client's trial up."

"Your Honour if they cancel another trial, could they slot us in?"

The judge raised her head in resignation after she rifled through some papers. "Okay, if an opening comes up, we'll see what we can do."

From the back, Paul's shoulder's slumped forward. Was it relief or resignation? The man couldn't decide.

A murmur rose in the courtroom and Paul glanced back. Nothing more than reporters getting restless with the mumbo jumbo of the process. They wanted to get at the news. Speculation about guilt would be the topic for months to come.

Paul's eyes locked with his. He lifted his ball cap to his head and peered down the row he'd have to squeeze through to reach the centre aisle and exit the courtroom. Their eyes had locked for only a split second. He rose to leave, but his heart stopped as Paul leaned over and whispered in April Somersby's ear, causing her to scan the courtroom behind her. The man let the door close heavily behind him. The excitement outside the courtroom quickly died when the reporters realized it was a man of no consequence.

The man stuck to the shadows, avoiding the cameras. No one watched him. They focused on the door, waiting for it to open again.

He smiled to himself. He strode out of the courthouse and slid into his Honda undetected. Time to call headquarters with the update of Paul's plea.

*****

Paul turned to show April the man at the back of the courtroom.

"Ms. Somersby, is there something more interesting at the back of the courtroom than what I have to say?"

Paul and April turned back. "No, your Honour, my apologies."

Paul's heart thudded in his chest. *A year. How will I survive a year before a trial?* But at the back of his mind, he wondered further. How would he survive many years in jail for a crime he never committed?

The judge rambled on about the process, but Paul couldn't listen. Why had Sam White shown up in court? Was his presence and the attempts on Paul's life related? Was he out to get him? Maybe he should have listened to him. Tried to get off through gang connections.

April touched his arm and he rose to his feet as the judge left the courtroom. She turned and grabbed his shoulder. "Now listen, Paul, we're going to get this trial moved up. Waiving the preliminary inquiry means we've made it easier to get slotted into a cancelled trial space. I'll be watching the docket carefully.

Paul nodded, but acid rose in the back of his mouth, and his stomach bubbled. He couldn't wait a year for justice to be served. This needed to be over soon.

He turned to the gallery and locked eyes with Nora. Zoe sat next to her. They held hands. Nora used her free hand to dab at her eyes. She pursed her lips, trying to smile for his sake, but unable to. The bailiff grabbed his elbow and steered him out of the courtroom. He hung his head and didn't glance back.

He stared at his shoes; shiny black, and freshly polished.

CONSEQUENCES

Was this the beginning of the end?

Lori Trembley. She always had caused him trouble, but never intentionally. She'd befriended him and they'd shared a bed a time or two, but trouble always followed them. Her dark brown eyes haunted him for years. And her last words echoed in his head. "You're better than this, Paul."

Those words turned his life around. Or was it her murder? Maybe both.

The overhead lights reflected in his shoes as he walked to the loading bay. He climbed into the van that would transport him back to jail. He peered out of the darkened windows, hoping to catch another glimpse of Nora and Zoe, but the crowd gathered at the front of the courthouse. April's pink blouse stood out as a beacon from the front steps through the throng of reporters. They'd be hungry to get any tidbit of news from her. But he trusted her not to say anything she shouldn't.

The van stopped at a red light and he peered into the car waiting in the lane beside them. It was a Honda, but he couldn't see the driver. He rested his head against the window, closed his eyes and imagined a world where Zoe hadn't posted her DNA results to GENmatch. A world he once grasped, but now slid from his reach. It had devastated Zoe when she learned of his arrest. His heart ached at the memory of Nora telling him about her sobs on the other end of the phone. She said she'd done it on a whim. Another friend had tested their DNA and found a sibling they never knew they had. When her DNA results came back, she posted the results to GENmatch. It's how she'd find connections with people who tested through other companies. She'd forgotten all about it and hadn't checked it in months. It was during that time the police posted their DNA results and found her as a match. Through her public family tree, they could discern who Paul was and locate him.

The van slowed to a stop before the gates opened, and he watched the prison come into view. He swallowed the lump in his throat and ran his handcuffed hands through his hair. The back door opened, and he stood as two guards grabbed his forearms and helped him to the ground.

The sun poured down. He turned his face upward to get the full effect, before the metal door clanged shut behind him. The smell of disinfectant mixed with sweat and dust settled around him. The lump rose once again, and he swallowed it back down. He concentrated on his breathing until at last he entered his cell and collapsed on the bed. Tears streamed down his cheeks, and he allowed them to fall. Maybe if he got it out of his system, he'd think more clearly.

CHAPTER TWENTY-THREE
April 13, 2018

April glanced at her phone. She'd agree to a date where David picked her up. She'd given him her address earlier in the day and he said he'd be there at seven-thirty on the dot; he was late.

Sorry, running behind. Be there in ten.

April shook her head and set her phone down. She despised tardiness. It meant people didn't respect her time. Did he think her time wasn't as valuable as his? She'd offered to meet him at the restaurant, but he insisted on picking her up, so she relented and gave him her address.

She took another look at her figure in the mirror. Was it too much? He had mentioned he'd like to see her in a little black dress. And this was the shortest one she owned. Tight fitting, it hugged the curves she worked so hard to keep in check.

She wandered into the kitchen, set her heels and purse by the front door and settled on the couch, scrolling through her phone.

She mindlessly glanced at photos of friends on Instagram. Friends with their kids, grandkids, partners. The life she missed out on in exchange for a law career. Was she that hard to live with? That bull headed? She glanced at the clock, and her anger rose. Maybe she was too hard headed. Too unbending. Is that why she was single at forty-nine?

A slamming car door brought her back to reality. She glanced out the window before proceeding to the front door and slipping on her heels. She opened the door before he had time to ring the bell.

"There's no excuse for being late. I'm so sorry. Truly, I am. I hate it when people are late." David pecked April on the side of the neck and placed a hand on her back before following her down the front steps.

April swallowed, then forced a smile. She needed to learn to bend. "Thought maybe I'd been stood up. After ducking out on you that first night, I'd deserve that."

David flashed the smile that attracted her to him, and she relented. If he didn't make tardiness a habit, she'd forgive him this one.

She slid into the front seat of his Aston Martin, the soft leather welcoming her as David pulled the seatbelt forward and handed it to her. She paused, staring up into his eyes, before clipping the seat belt and watching him scoot around the front of the car and slide into the driver's seat. *What am I worrying about? So what if he was late?*

*****

"Scotch neat and another glass of wine." David pointed to April's glass and winked at the waitress, who blushed, and pranced toward the bar with a wiggle showing off her perky twenty-something physique in the mini-skirt. April noticed David didn't watch the waitress walk away. He was too busy staring at her.

"What?" April blushed and downed the rest of the wine in her glass.

"Nothing, nothing at all. Just enjoying the view." His eyes twinkled even under the dim lights.

Chills crawled up April's spine, and she shivered.

"Cold?"

"No, I was just thinking about something."

David sat back in his chair, the corners of his mouth hinting at a smile.

She knew he was aware of the effect he had on her. She rarely let anyone see her that vulnerable. But somehow this seemed okay. "This dinner's been a long time in the making so I hate to even suggest it, but why don't we take a meal back to my place?"

David's eyes widened, and he leaned forward. "Are you sure about that?"

"I have a good feeling about you."

The waitress dropped off the drinks and took their food

order for takeaway. Not something they were likely used to doing in this type of establishment.

David leaned forward, one hand on his drink and the other over April's hand on the table. "I'm sure you don't want to talk about work, but I saw on the news your client pleaded not guilty and waived his preliminary hearing. You don't see that very often. Someone on murder charges waiving the preliminary, do you?"

"I don't want to talk about work. But you're right, murder trial preliminaries don't get waived too often. My client needs to get this trial moved up. He can't wait another year in jail. They've attacked him twice. Gang ties mean he could still be at risk. We just want this trial over. He's innocent, and I'm hoping we can create enough doubt to get him off. If there's a cancellation, the judge said she'd bump up the trial. I'm crossing my fingers for that." April observed David. It was nice to have someone interested in what she did. Too often guys just wanted to talk about what they did for a living, making her feel inconsequential.

"Okay, enough talk about work. Tell me who you really are, April Somersby?" David leaned back and raised his glass to his lips.

"Oh, just a small-town girl trying to make it in the big city."

"Well, I'd say you made it alright. Look at you. Big profile case. Where did you come from?" David reached for his scotch, taking another sip while keeping his other hand on hers.

"Oh, you've likely never heard of it. A place in Saskatchewan called Outlook."

"Nope, can't say I have. How'd you end up in Vancouver?"

April felt like she was droning on, monopolizing the conversation, but he kept turning the topic back on her. It was nice to have someone interested in her for a change.

At last, the waitress showed up with their dinner bagged and ready to go. They downed their drinks, and he paid for the meal, although April tried to insist on paying her share.

"I need to use the restroom. Do you mind?"

"Not at all. I'll wait at the front of the restaurant."

Am I really doing this? It had been a long time since she invited anyone back to her place. She ducked into the washroom and stood in front of the mirror. What did he see in her? He was gorgeous. She was ordinary. In a crowd, she wouldn't stand out. Yet somehow, he'd picked her.

Quit being so hard on yourself. Her colleagues were always telling her she sold herself short. Maybe he really was attracted to her. She smeared on some lipstick and stood staring at herself for another moment. Maybe this was the relationship she'd been searching for.

She shouldered her purse, straightened and strode out of the restroom with the confidence she knew she had. David stood at the door, waiting for her. They rode in silence to her house.

David jumped out of the car as soon as they arrived and was at her door, opening it as she unclipped her seatbelt. He carried dinner and followed her up the walk. She opted to use the front door for a change. He held the screen door as she fumbled with the key.

"It's nothing special, but I like it." She wasn't sure why she was apologizing for owning a home in Vancouver. Real estate was expensive. She'd bought years before the market skyrocketed, and she could get a fortune for it. But it was home and she had no intention of selling.

"I love it. David paused inside the door, handing her the bags once she'd removed her jacket.

"There's a spare hanger in the closet." April set the bags on the island and reached into the cupboard to pull down plates and cutlery. David reached over her head and grabbed two wine glasses. That shiver escaped her again.

He placed his hand on her, and she turned to face him.

"April Somersby. I'm not sure I'm all that hungry." His lips touched hers and April set the plates down. When he pulled away, she slid her hand in his and led him down the hall to the bedroom.

CHAPTER TWENTY-FOUR
April 14, 2018

Paul tapped the table with his index finger and glanced up at the clock. Nora was visiting less and less often. He understood. It must be hard for her to see him in jail. If it was the other way around, though, he'd be there every day.

His finger stopped its bouncing motion as Nora strode across the room. Had she lost weight? Her hair and minimal makeup were the same perfection she always strived for, but her clothes seemed to hang off her petite frame. And the worry behind her eyes pierced Paul's heart.

"How's Zoe? How are you?"

The conversation always started the same way. He was desperate for outside news. Anything. But Nora's responses were terse. She didn't seem to have much news for him. Each visit was a little more awkward.

"Oh fine. She's coming home for the summer. Did I already

tell you that?" Nora sat with her hands in her jacket pockets.

"You did. I bet you're excited. It'll be good to have her with you. But what about you? How are you doing, Nora? He leaned forward, placing his hands on the table.

"Well, I'd have to say, I've felt better, Paul." The worry behind her eyes blazed with anger.

"What do you mean, what's wrong?" Paul sat straight, catching the guard step forward out of the corner of his eye. He settled back into his chair, his eyes never leaving Nora's face.

She continued to stare into his soul, then cleared her throat. "I was doing spring cleaning and came across a few things."

"Oh, what things? Old photos or something? Boy, I'd love to go through that old box of photos with you. I'm sure we'd have a lot of laughs." His chuckle fell flat with her unrelenting stare.

"No, not photos. I cleaned out our closet. Donated some items to charity." She paused as if she didn't know how to proceed.

Paul inhaled deeply. Afraid of what she was about to say.

"At the back of the closet, I found an old shoe box. I'd never noticed it before. A pile of things on the shelf on your side hidden from view."

Paul bowed his head and stared at his hands in his lap. A lump formed in the back of his throat. He knew what box she was talking about. The box he thought the police would find when they searched his house after he was arrested. But they never did. He raised his head.

Nora stared from behind angry, haunted eyes, clearing her throat before continuing. "I'm sure you know the one I'm talking about?"

Paul nodded almost imperceptibly and licked his lips. "You mean that Adidas shoebox with a bunch of odds and ends?"

Nora nodded, but remained silent.

"Yeah, I kept that to remind me of the life I left behind and why I never want to go back." He fidgeted in his seat, then forced himself to sit straighter.

Nora took a deep breath. Her face was a mixture of emotions. Tears welled up, but never overflowed. She coughed and blinked away the tears. They sat in silence.

Finally, Paul leaned forward. "It's been so long since I've looked in there. What did you find?"

Nora straightened, but her gaze dropped to the table. "A few old papers, some badges; maybe gang badges?"

Paul grinned. "Oh, yeah. Other people enrolled in boy scouts. I enrolled in the Clark Park gang. Not quite the same type of badge collecting." His grin faded when Nora didn't smile back. "I take it you found something else as well? What'd you find, Nora?"

Nora glanced around the room, then slid something across the table to him. The guard's attention focused on someone entering the room. Paul slid the paper off of the table and into his lap.

A tear escaped and slid down Nora's cheek. She swiped at it before rising and walking toward the door. Paul glanced into his lap, but knew without looking exactly what it was. "Nora, wait."

She didn't turn around before leaving the room. Paul clasped the paper in his hand and rose. The guard's boots echoed off the cement walls on the walk back to his cell. When the door clanged shut and the lock clicked into place, he stood still, the newspaper article heavy in his hand. What it said wasn't something he ever forgot.

Paul laid down on his bed facing the wall and unfolded the paper. He raised it to his face and inhaled the musty odour of old newsprint before he opened his eyes and read the familiar headline, *Murder Victim Identified as Lori Trembley*. There was no mistaking the clipping dated the day after the murder. His heart raced. Why had he kept it? Deep down, he knew it wasn't something he ever wanted Nora or Zoe knowing about. But it meant something to him. He cut it out of the paper that day and slid it into his wallet, where he stored it for the next two years. Her death hit him hard. It turned his life around. She was a good person. Under different circumstances, maybe they could have straightened each other out. Maybe he could have helped her escape the gang life she was born into.

But instead, she died, and now they accused him of killing her. Did Nora see the clipping as a trophy, an admission of guilt? Paul closed his eyes, holding the paper against his chest under the palm of his hand. Tears stung the back of his eyelids.

His heart thumped in his chest and his breathing came in quick gasps. He'd lost Nora's trust. April was right, he needed to come clean. Let her know everything. Or at least almost everything.

*****

The sunlight snuck down the hall from windows Paul couldn't see. He waited in the visitor centre for the second day in a row. He was well aware of Nora's reason for coming again so soon. She wanted an explanation, and he'd rehearsed his reason for the newspaper clipping all morning. He glanced at the clock. What was taking so long for her to be screened?

Then the door opened, and Nora walked across the floor. Not tentatively. Not excitedly. She strode in with confidence. Like someone on a mission.

Paul shifted in his chair. Nora settled in across from him; back straight, and staring into his eyes.

"Listen honey, I want to explain." Paul leaned forward, palms holding down the table.

Nora silenced him with a wave of her hand. "No, you listen to me. I've had enough of your games. It's time you told the entire story." She glanced around, then lowered her voice to a whisper. "You knew Lori Trembley?"

The ache in her voice reached inside Paul and gripped his heart. He nodded and avoided her eyes by staring down at the table. He straightened his shoulders, then raised his eyes until they gazed into his wife's. "I knew her. She was a friend. Maybe more than a friend."

Nora's eyebrows raised, but her gaze remained consistent.

"I knew her from the gang days in the seventies. She was the sister of a rival gang member. Paul glanced around the room before leaning forward and lowering his voice. The

Riley Parkers. Her brothers wouldn't allow us to see each other, but sometimes we met up. She was a nice person trapped in a dangerous situation. She and her brothers ended up in another gang after the Riley Parkers dissolved." Paul took a deep breath, hoping Nora would say something, but she remained silent.

"I would never have hurt a hair on her head. I think maybe at one time I even thought I loved her."

Nora's eyes widened.

"But that was before you. Hell, she died before we met. What was there for me to tell you about her? I had a friend I cared about who was a member of a gang and killed before I met you? We needed a fresh start. I didn't want my past hanging over us."

Nora leaned forward. "Yet here we are. Your past and Lori Trembley hanging over us, between us, ruining our lives. Why did you keep the clipping all these years, Paul?"

Nora's eyes cut through his soul. Her doubt, her fear, stabbing right through him.

"I don't know. I haven't looked in the box for years. If I had, I would have thrown out the clipping. Initially I kept it because her murder made me sad and angry. Angry that I hadn't protected her. Sad because she was someone, I thought I loved. I couldn't let go of her, and that clipping was all I had. Not a great explanation, I know."

Nora leaned back and exhaled. "Did you keep a clipping of your parent's death too?"

"Yeah, for a time. But I lost it a couple of years later when

148

my wallet was stolen. Paul tightened his fists. "Please believe me, Nora. I had nothing to do with her murder. It devastated me." His eyes implored her to believe him.

At last, her face softened. "You should have told me long ago. At the very least, the day they took you for that damn DNA test."

Paul nodded. "I know. I'm sorry. Truly sorry."

"Do you still have the clipping?"

Paul glanced around the room and leaned forward. "No, I flushed it down the toilet yesterday. I'll tell April about my connection to Lori. And I'll tell her about the clipping.

"Okay, good. Because if you don't, I will. If you're innocent, Paul, you need to be upfront with me and your lawyer. Maybe the truth will become clear for everyone to see."

Paul smiled, but deep down, he wondered if coming clean would just ensure he never saw the outside of a jail cell again.

"If you knew her that well, do you have any idea who murdered her?"

The hope in Nora's eyes crushed him.

"No one in particular. I heard on the streets it was a contract killing ordered by another gang. But I distanced myself from gangs, straightened myself out and got clean. I met you soon after and you were my reason for living."

An audible sigh reached Paul from the other side of the table. He felt the tension in his back release. Nora believed him.

CHAPTER TWENTY-FIVE
April 15, 2018

"You knew Lori Trembley?" April sat across from Paul, shaking her head. Her pen stopped moving across the paper in front of her. "Three months after arraignment, and you're now telling me you knew the victim you're accused of killing?"

Paul hung his head and nodded, raising his eyes to meet hers. "Yeah, I knew Lori Trembley well."

"I think you better explain that to me. How well?" April's pen was back in the poised position.

"I knew her in the early 70s during my Clark Park days. She was the sister to a Riley Park member, so we didn't exactly socialize. But there was an attraction. Then I ran into her in the early 90s and we still hit it off. Neither of us had a partner, so occasionally we shared a bed. She became embedded in gang life, dealing drugs, and although I slid back into old habits, I never joined a gang."

April's pen moved furiously over the page, and Paul paused to let her catch up before continuing. "I crashed at her place when I was too slammed to get home. She took care of me on many occasions. She was a good friend." Paul sipped water from the plastic glass in front of him.

"What gang did she belong to?" April flexed her hand before poising it on the paper in front of her once again.

"I believe it was Big Circle Boys."

April inhaled sharply. "You believe, or you know?"

"I know. She told me herself."

"Did she also tell you who her enemies were?"

"No. We never talked about her gang ties or what she did. I mean, I knew what she did, but it wasn't something we talked about." Paul paused, then continued. "We reminisced about the good old days. The days when being a gang member didn't include carrying a gun."

"So, she carried a gun?"

"Oh, I have no idea. Probably. It was just known that in the 90s, the gang culture had evolved to much higher levels of danger and gun violence wasn't uncommon."

April stopped writing and laid her pen down. "Okay, Paul, I need you to focus. Focus on the day Lori Trembley died. I know you've said you don't know where you were, but really? If she meant that much to you, you'd remember. Where were you?"

Silence filled the room. Paul cleared his throat. "I was at my apartment recovering."

April's eye widened, and she shrugged. "Recovering from what?"

"A couple of things. A really terrible hangover and a stab wound to my arm."

April leaned back for a moment before repositioning her pen. "Okay, just come out with it, Paul. I shouldn't have to pull the story out of you. I'm here to help you, remember?"

"It's just hard for me to talk about. I'm not proud of the person I was in those days, and I've never talked to anyone about that day or the day before. Not even Nora."

"Just take your time and let it out. I need to hear it."

Paul inhaled. It was time. "The day before Lori was killed, I was in a bar fight. Someone stabbed me in the arm, and I was lucky it wasn't worse. It was the third day of a bender and it's all a bit foggy. But I do remember stumbling into Lori's place late that night. She cleaned me up and even threw in a couple of stitches. I crashed on her couch. She woke me about noon and told me to leave because she had some things to take care of. I was in a foul mood. We fought. The last words she said to me were, 'You're better than this, Paul.'"

Paul's words lingered on waves of silence.

He slouched in his chair and ran a hand through his hair. "Those words have echoed in my head ever since. I was angry with her, but after I learned of her murder, I vowed to live up to them."

"You were in her apartment the day she was murdered?" April's pen had stopped moving and her mouth hung open, wide eyes transfixed on Paul.

"Yes."

April shook her head in disbelief. "So, when did you hear about her death?"

"It wasn't till the next day when the police released her name on the news. After I left her place, I stumbled home and fell into bed. I didn't wake until the next day. I took an Advil and turned on the news at noon. Her face flashed on the screen, and the Advil came up with the little stomach contents I had left."

April's voice cracked. "You were with her? In her apartment on the day she was murdered, and you didn't think that was important to tell me?"

Paul stared at the table.

"Okay, sorry I just can't believe you've held all this from me." April bounced the pen on the pad of paper. Silence fell between them.

"Okay, I realize her death must have been hard on you." April exhaled before continuing. "Did you reach out to anybody at that time?"

"Not initially. I think I stayed indoors for a couple of days. Grieving. Trying to make sense of it. Feeling terrible about our fight. Worrying someone might have seen me going in or out of Lori's place. That I'd get blamed and the Big Circle Boys would come after me. But I heard the rumours that a rival gang member shot her. She'd ventured into someone else's territory dealing drugs. People assumed it was a gang contract killing."

"Let's back up a bit. You were in Lori's place the morning of her murder, wounded?"

Paul shifted in his seat and hung his head. "Yeah. I know I should have told you sooner, but I'm ashamed of so much of my past. It's hard to talk about any of it."

April sighed, refusing to fill the silence.

"But don't get any ideas about my blood on her floor. If there were any drops of blood, she'd have cleaned them up." Paul sat forward. "I wish I could say I left my blood everywhere. But she worked on the wound in her kitchen and bandaged it well. I hadn't even bled through the bandage when I got up a day later in my place."

April's face dropped. "But it's possible she missed some blood?"

"Not in the living room by the coffee table. I didn't bleed there."

"I'm going to focus on you bleeding in her apartment the day of her murder. Placing you at the scene might backfire, but it explains how your blood may be there. I have to use it."

Paul shook his head and swallowed. "Do we really have to bring it up?"

"Their only piece of evidence is your DNA at the scene. We have to explain it. This does. I wish you had an alibi for where you were the rest of that day and the days following.

You're sure no one came to visit you at your apartment or you didn't go out?"

Paul shook his head. "No, I was home alone."

April closed her notepad and rested her hands on the table. "Thank you for telling me, Paul. I'm not going to lie. I'm angry it's taken you this long to come clean. But I have good news for you."

Paul's eyes brightened.

"They've moved your trial up because of a cancellation. We have a month to finish preparing."

Paul smiled, but acid rose in his throat. This was what he wanted, right? To get it over with. But what if they couldn't create doubt? What if placing him at the scene created more probability rather than explaining away his DNA? And with gang members everywhere, he wouldn't survive more than a few days if he was released into prison general population.

CHAPTER TWENTY-SIX
April 15, 2018

The man poured himself a bourbon and settled into the leather chair, rested his feet on the overstuffed ottoman, and contemplated the room. He'd settled in, but he looked forward to returning home. Surely the information he had would placate the client.

He took a deep breath and dialed, resting his drink on the glass side table. He shivered as he remembered the glass coffee table at Lori Trembley's house.

"What do you have for me?" The voice on the other end of the phone was clear. Blunt. All business.

The man straightened in his chair and removed his feet from the ottoman, resting them on the floor. "Reporting in on the case.

The man heard the squeak of an office chair straightening. He needed to get to the point. "Nothing new. But I'm wondering if you told the client about the hair evidence?"

The man's heart pounded. It was time to get back to making money, instead of losing it over a case he'd already taken care of.

"I did, but like I told you, unless Paul Giovanni is found not guilty, you'll never get another job."

"I know. But with the hair evidence, I'm confident they'll find Paul innocent."

"Perhaps. But the blood of Paul Giovanni suggests he was there too. If I were you, I'd be looking for other evidence or holes in the case."

The line went silent, and the man let his phone drop in his lap. He reached over for his drink, swirling it and staring at the amber liquid before tipping it back and downing the whole glass.

"Damn it!" His voice echoed in the empty suite. The client was being very unreasonable. This was a perfect storm. The police wouldn't look for him if Paul was convicted. If only it wasn't Paul, maybe he could retire. But he owed Paul.

He shook his head, and a grin hinted at the corners of his mouth. When he sat in front of Paul in the visitor centre there might have been the slightest hint of recognition, but Paul hadn't put it together. That was fortunate. But in some ways, sad. How could he not recognize him?

He reached for the remote and turned on the TV. Susan Ormsby stared back at him.

"Recent developments in the Lori Trembley cold case. The

courts have expedited Paul Giovanni's trial to next month. The speed of this trial is virtually unheard of these days..."

A smile crept across the man's face. The timing of this news was perfect. He rose and poured himself another finger of bourbon. He could handle another month. He hoped April Somersby was up to the task.

CHAPTER TWENTY-SEVEN
May 11, 2018

April glanced at her phone.

Dinner?

Seven o'clock and she hadn't lifted her head since noon. Her stomach grumbled, but her gaze landed on the stack of papers on the corner of the desk.

Sorry, swamped. Rain check?

Unease settled around her. Was she sabotaging the only genuine relationship she'd had in a decade? With the trial expedited and other cases piling up, work had to come first.

It was a few minutes before a response appeared.

You have to eat. How about I bring dinner? I promise to leave as soon as we're done. The break will do you good.

April breathed a sigh of relief. He was so understanding.

I'm still at the office. If it's not too much bother, that would be wonderful.

She dove back into the paperwork, and what seemed like only moments later, her phone dinged. David was downstairs.

The smell of Italian food wafted into the lobby. He reached down, moving a tendril of hair before kissing her cheek. "You look exhausted. Maybe some primavera will perk you up."

"You don't know how much I needed this break. Thank you for coming by and for being so understanding. It smells delicious." April swiped her card in the elevator and pressed the 8th floor button.

The doors slid closed and David leaned over, covering her lips with his. A tingle rode up her spine before she turned her head. "You don't know how much I wish we could continue, but I have work to do. If you keep this up, I'll forget all about it."

David cleared his throat and leaned his head against the wall. "Sorry. I'm not helping. I promise I'll keep my distance."

The elevator doors opened and April led the way to the boardroom. David pulled out the feast, complete with plastic utensils and paper plates. April filled her plate first and David followed, sitting next to her.

"So, how's the case coming? Can't imagine how busy it is now that the trial's moved up. Are you feeling good about it?"

April smiled weakly and shrugged. "There's been something new that's come to light. Wish I could talk about it, but I can't. I really do need to bounce it off someone though."

"I understand and I'd love to help." David scooped up a fork full of primavera, juggling it with the plastic utensil. "Next time I'll buy real silverware. Hey, could you make it a hypothetical situation? I mean you could talk about a hypothetical case, couldn't you?"

April twirled the pasta with her fork, contemplating David's offer to help. She knew in her heart she shouldn't pursue this, but she really did want his opinion on whether exposing Paul's relationship with Lori was a nail in the coffin or the break in the case they needed.

"Okay. Remember this is completely hypothetical. It has nothing to do with the current case, okay?"

David grinned and leaned back in his chair. "Got it."

April paused, thinking carefully of how to word her hypothetical situation. "Okay, here goes. A lawyer learns her client's had a relationship with the victim of the murder he's charged with. And that relationship places him at the crime scene on the day of the murder. The prosecution isn't aware of the relationship. Would you bring it up in court as it may explain how evidence of the defendant was found at the scene, or would you not reveal it? As a juror would..." April's words faded as she took in David's reaction, a slow grin spreading across his face. It wasn't the reaction she expected.

David cleared his throat, the grin disappearing from his face. "Go on."

April studied him carefully, then continued. "As a juror, would placing him at the scene to explain the evidence create doubt about the defendant's guilt, or would it cement it?"

"Woah. Now that's a dilemma." David leaned forward. "Hypothetically, was the defendant bleeding at the scene? Was there any evidence that might prove anyone else was at the scene?"

April sighed, pushing her plate away and lowered her eyes. "Hypothetically, yes."

"Then, yes, as a juror, I think it has the potential to create doubt in my mind. Of course, it may also create questions about motive. If you can address motive concerns, I would definitely see it creating doubt in a juror's mind. Why did it take the defendant so long to admit to a relationship with the defendant?"

April grinned. "Who said it took a long time?"

"Oh right, hypothetical. So hypothetically, say it did take a long time. Why?"

"Oh, I don't know. Perhaps his wife found evidence that pointed to a relationship and she confronted him with it?"

David nodded. "I see. The old wife guilt trip; works every time."

"Thanks for playing along, but I think enough has been said. Remember, this hypothetical conversation never happened."

"What conversation?" David reached into the paper bag

pulling out a tray of tiramisu. I take it you're ready for dessert?"

"Oh, you know the way to a girl's heart."

David winked and April wondered if it was the tic or if he meant it that time.

They finished their dessert in awkward silence, both thinking about the conversation that never happened. Finally, David rose and packed up the containers, plates, and cutlery, then sat back and stared into April's eyes.

"I promised I'd let you get back to work. Are you okay? Truly you've nothing to worry about. Our conversation never happened. Want to accompany me down to the front door?"

"No, but I will." April grinned and rose from her chair. As the elevator doors closed, a tingle climbed April's spine again, and she felt her face grow hot at the thought of the passion he'd shown her on the trip up. She let out an audible sigh.

"I know. I feel the same way." David smiled and squeezed her hand.

She watched him walk out to his red Aston Martin, then turned and rode the elevator up again. Elevator rides would never be the same.

CHAPTER TWENTY-EIGHT
May 12, 2018

Stakeouts were nothing new to him. He'd done them dozens of times. They usually ended with someone dying. This time was different.

He watched Nora and Zoe Giovanni back out of the driveway. Zoe exited the front door with reusable bags while Nora backed the car out of the garage. With those bags, he assumed they'd gone grocery shopping, which should give him at least an hour. Enough time to get a lay of the land. People hid things in the same places. Under mattresses, in dresser drawers and closet shelves.

He didn't know what he was looking for, but he hoped he'd find something to help Paul Giovanni. There had to be something to help prove his innocence.

Trees blocked the view of the front door from the street, giving him the cover, he needed. He popped the lock in less than five seconds and closed the door quickly behind him.

Perfume lingered in the air and he paused to listen. The fridge hummed, the air conditioning kicked in and the dishwasher reached the end of its cycle and drained. No other creaks or noises to indicate anyone else occupied the house.

He climbed the staircase beside the entrance. Bedrooms were typically on the second floor. The door at the top of the stairs hung open. He glanced in. A bathroom. The next room's door was ajar, and he pushed it open. A single bed with clothes strewn across the floor. Vanity with makeup and blow dryer littering the surface. And the sweet scent of perfume was stronger, almost overpowering. Clearly Zoe's room. He adjusted the door to where it had been, not that anyone would notice a few inches, but he was meticulous.

He paused, putting his ear to the door at the end of the hallway before opening. A king-size bed was the focal point of the room. Two large dressers lined the wall, with a door on the right. He pulled open the bottom drawer in the long dresser with the mirror. Lady's sweaters lay folded in piles. He closed the drawer without investigating and moved over to the tallboy. The bottom drawer held men's jeans, also neatly folded. He ran a gloved hand under the jeans, reaching to the far corners of the drawer. Nothing. The other four drawers didn't reveal anything either. Straightening the piles before closing the drawers, he turned his attention to the door, opening it to reveal a walk-in closet, impeccably clean. Even the odds and ends on the shelves above were orderly.

He glanced around and found the step stool he knew must be nearby. Nora was not a tall woman and if there's one thing he'd learned after all his stakeouts, it was short women have stools handy. He unfolded the stool and climbed onto the top step. He looked for dust. There was none. His gaze went up further to a shoebox with tattered corners sitting in the far corner of the top shelf. He moved the stool so he could reach the box and pulled it from the shelf. Stepping off the stool, he placed the box on the top step and lifted the lid. The badges caught his eye first. He recognized them as gang badges from the seventies. Old student identification cards littered the bottom of the box and he lifted each one out. The last card caused him to pause.

His heart pounded in his chest and he turned the card over. Old memories stirred and his overwhelming feeling of gratitude to Paul Giovanni washed over him. Something told him this card might be important. It was, after all, the only link he and Paul had. The thought created a wedge, peeling back an idea, a niggle. Something he needed to mull over. He slipped the card into his pocket and checked his watch. It had been thirty-five minutes. He slid the box back into its spot on the shelf. At least with no dust, he didn't have to worry about leaving marks. He replaced the stool, scanned the room and backed out, closing the door behind him.

It was when he hit the landing that he heard the garage door open. He sprinted down the stairs and peeked out the front curtain. The car slid into the garage. They were back sooner than he'd anticipated. He let himself out, relocked the door, and casually walked up the sidewalk and across the street to his car. He waited until the garage door closed before he pulled away from the curb.

His knee steadied the wheel as he peeled off his gloves and placed them in the console. He reached into his right jacket pocket and rubbed the card. A news story from a couple years earlier flashed across his mind. *Why didn't I think of it earlier?*

CHAPTER TWENTY-NINE
May 15, 2018

Paul shuffled into the courtroom, a bailiff at his side. The aroma of polished wood permeated his senses. The room buzzed with low voices that seemed to pause as he entered, then continue in a slightly heightened hum. He glanced at the gallery, his gaze falling on Nora and Zoe in the front row. They stared at him, expressions trying to convey hopefulness, but instead appeared desperate. He tore his gaze away and turned to sit in the wooden chair beside April at the defendant's table. He'd glanced at the prosecution upon entering the room, but quickly looked away. His stomach turned at the thought of the days that stretched ahead and the prosecution's goal to put him away for life.

The day before, the trial began with opening remarks. The prosecution painted a bleak picture. April tried to insert doubt into their case, but Paul couldn't see how a jury would acquit him with the DNA evidence presented. She painted a picture of an upstanding citizen, hard worker, trustworthy member of society. But that was now, not then. The prosecution would have to be daft not to bring up his sordid past, which would negate all the work he'd done to try to erase it.

April patted the back of his hand. Her face did reflect hope, but she tried too hard. The ball in the pit of his stomach turned.

"Please rise. The Honourable Judge Alisha Monroe presiding."

Paul pushed his chair back and stood. He scanned the jury.

April fidgeted and muttered under her breath. "Too many women." Seven out of twelve were female. She'd tried her best to get more males than females on the jury, but the judge intervened, citing her for using her peremptory challenges based on gender. She tried to argue, but the judge shut her down.

Paul lowered himself into his chair and placed a hand on his jittery knee. April had advised him not to show emotion or nerves to the jury. It would need to be his best acting to get through the trial.

The prosecution rose. "Your Honour we'd like to call our first witness, Joe Walters."

Paul watched his friend make his way to the witness stand. His eyes held Paul's for a short time. Long enough for Paul to see regret.

Joe raised his right hand and swore to tell the truth, then sat down. Paul wouldn't have recognized him if he'd met him on the street. His short hair and a well-trimmed moustache held a bit of grey. He'd grown from a misfit into a handsome man with chiseled features.

"Mr. Walters, how long were you a police officer before you retired?

Joe became a policeman? Paul shook his head and grinned. He would never have guessed that's where Joe would end up.

"Twenty-five years."

"Always with the Vancouver City Police?"

"Yes."

"As a youth, were you a member of the Clark Park Gang in Vancouver?"

"Yes. I was twelve and thirteen years old."

"And did you know Paul Giovanni then?"

"Yes."

"Would you say you were friends?"

"Yes."

Paul's knee shook and April shot him a sideways glance.

"Was Paul also a Clark Park Gang member?"

Joe cleared his throat. "Yes."

"And did you know Lori Trembley?"

Silence filled the courtroom.

"Please answer the question, Mr. Walters."

Paul held his breath.

"Yes."

"Can you please explain to the jury how you knew Lori Trembley?"

Paul didn't want it to play out this way. April was supposed to bring out how he knew Lori, not the prosecution.

"She was the sister of a Riley Park member. I saw her around now and again."

"Did you ever date her?"

"No."

"Did your friend Paul know her?"

April rose to her feet. "Objection, your Honour. Speculative."

Judge Munroe leaned forward. "Sustained."

The prosecution paused and turned to the defence table. "Did you ever see your friend Paul with Lori Trembley?"

Paul held his breath. Had Joe ever seen them together?

Joe appeared stoic, unphased, except his ashen complexion gave away the turmoil he felt inside.

"No, I never saw Paul with Lori Trembley."

Joe met Paul's gaze, and Paul could swear he saw the hint of a smile. He clasped his trembling hands under the table.

The prosecutor turned to stare at his witness. Joe simply stared back.

"No more questions, your Honour."

April rose and crossed the floor. "Do you mind if I call you Joe?"

"Not at all."

"Would you categorize Paul as your best friend when you joined the Clark Parkers at twelve years old?"

"Yes."

"Did you see Paul after 1972, when the Clark Park Gang disbanded?"

"No."

"What happened to you after the gang disbanded?"

"I straightened out. Unlike Paul, I came from a good home with supportive parents. After Paul's parents died and he went into foster care, I never saw or heard from him again."

"How would you categorize Paul's character in those days?"

Joe stared at Paul. An unspoken sadness crossing the room. "He was a good kid in a bad situation. His dad was a drunk.

His mom worked hard to make up for it. He joined the gang for protection. All the young kids did."

"As a police officer in the 90s, did you ever encounter Lori Trembley?"

"Yes. We brought her in for questioning once in relation to a drug deal gone bad. But we never arrested her."

"And were you aware she was a member of the Big Circle Gang?"

The prosecutor jumped to his feet. "Speculation, your Honour."

April turned to the judge. "It's only speculation if he wasn't a police officer, and didn't know the gang members in the nineties."

"Overruled. Answer the question Mr. Walters."

"Yes. We suspected she was part of the Big Circle Gang."

"And from your dealings with gangs in the nineties, would you say murders were common between rival gangs?"

"Yes. It was one of our priorities to stop gang violence."

"Thank you. Your Honour, I have no further questions."

April smiled at Paul as she strode back to the defence table. Joe rose from the stand, and Paul nodded as Joe walked by. He could have sworn Joe did the same thing.

"Your Honour, we call Dr. Brent Carlos to the stand."

They weren't wasting any time getting to the DNA evidence. Dr. Carlos strode up the aisle in his expensive business suit, swore his oath, and sat down. He had a calm demeanour about him. One even Paul trusted. Their eyes locked, but it wasn't a malicious stare. Rather, a curious one. As if Paul was a subject he wanted to study.

"Your Honour, I present Exhibit A into evidence, the results of the DNA test performed on the blood at the scene." The prosecutor approached the judge and placed a document on the bench. He returned to his table and retrieved a second document. "And your Honour, I present Exhibit B into evidence, the results from the DNA test performed on the defendant, Paul Giovanni." He approached the bench once again, depositing the second document.

Paul turned to the jurors. One woman stared directly at him, not lowering her gaze even when he stared back. Paul finally looked down.

"Your Honour. I'm going to project these documents onto the screen as Dr. Carlos explains the results. A projector whirred to life in the quiet courtroom and the two documents appeared on the screen. Paul tried to concentrate. Dr. Carlos droned on, comparing the bands on the screen and talking about centromeres. Paul tried to concentrate on what was being said, but it was like the words bled through a fog. It didn't take a genius to see the match between the two results. It was clear. The two samples were identical.

"So, Dr. Carlos, can you tell me beyond a reasonable doubt that the DNA in the blood at the scene of the murder of Lori Trembley on April 17, 1994 and the blood taken from Paul Giovanni are an exact match?"

"Yes. Both samples are from the same person."

Paul lowered his head and stared at the table in front of him. A gentle nudge from April brought him back. She'd told him to look straight ahead, not slouch and to appear confident. Not even an hour into day two and he'd lost focus. He pulled his shoulders back and raised his gaze.

*****

April rose and approached the witness stand. "Dr. Carlos, you say the two DNA samples are a perfect match. Is that correct?"

"Objection, your Honour. That has already been established."

April raised her hand in acknowledgement and continued. "Okay, Dr. Carlos. You've stated that the DNA in both samples is a perfect match. Tell me though…" April turned and strode toward the jury. "Can two people have identical DNA?" A few jurors straightened in their chairs.

The witness cleared his throat. The courtroom turned silent. "Well, yes, they can."

"So, you're telling me you can't say for certain this DNA belongs to the same person? Is that correct?" April stared at the jury. They were paying attention. One juror leaned forward. Clearly for this juror, things were getting interesting. April turned to Dr. Carlos.

"Correct. Sometimes two people have the same genes."

The courtroom erupted into a buzz. April glanced at Paul. He sat straight, emotionless. His leg still.

"When would two people carry the same genes?"

Dr. Carlos glanced at the prosecution bench before responding. "Identical twins have the same DNA."

April strode toward the defence bench, allowing the courtroom time to settle down. She pulled out her chair, but then, as if changing her mind, returned to the witness stand.

"Thank you, Dr. Carlos. One more question, if you don't mind. Can you tell me if hair is a valuable source of DNA at a crime scene?"

Again, Dr. Carlos looked toward the prosecution, perhaps expecting them to object, but they remained silent. "It can be. That depends."

April raised her eyebrows. "Depends on what?"

"It depends on how much is present, and whether the root of the hair is intact."

"Can you please explain that?"

"They can perform some DNA testing from the shaft of the hair, but the root of the hair provides more valuable and extensive information."

"If you had lots of hair at the scene with intact roots and a drop of blood, which would be a better source of DNA information?"

The prosecutor jumped to his feet. "Objection, your Honour. Supposition."

April stepped toward the bench. "Your Honour, the

evidence submitted by the prosecution contained information about hair found at the scene of the crime. I'm simply asking their expert witness to determine the validity of test results on hair versus blood."

"Overruled. Will the witness please answer the question?"

Dr. Carlos stared at the floor and cleared his throat before continuing. "Neither sample would negate the other. They're both valuable."

"Thank you, Dr. Carlos. I have no further questions."

April turned and strode back to the table, her heels clicking on the marble floor, taking a deep breath as she sat down. If nothing else, she caught the jury's attention. And that's what she'd set out to do. Paul didn't have an identical twin, or at least not one she was aware of, but it was a seed of doubt planted in the jurors' minds. The hair might help in the long run when she presented it as evidence, but it didn't remove Paul from the crime scene.

CHAPTER THIRTY
May 3, 1994

Paul sat hunched over on the side of his bed, his arms out in front of him, palms up. The TV blared out the latest news from the common room. A couple days after Lori's murder, he'd left his apartment and walked the streets until he wandered into a shelter that would take him. A couple of weeks later and he'd landed one of the coveted single rooms where it was easier to control the bedbugs. He counted the fading tracks in his arms and flopped backwards onto the bed.

What would his mother think? Maybe he wasn't any better than his old man, after all? Murder. He closed his eyes but couldn't shut out his mom, face down in a pool of blood, while his dad stared straight at the ceiling, the gash along his neck and the knife splayed out beside him. Everything else from that time was a blur except for the images of his parents. Lori's murder brought it all back to him.

Jane, his foster mom, took him in and gave him a home, an

education, and a second chance. She was a nurse at the transplant centre and taught him the value of an education. Showed him how he could escape his past. And he did. He built a life. Went to trades school, became a heavy-duty mechanic. He'd never had so much money in his life. Living in camp meant days off gave him time to party and spend that hard earned cash. He had the money to do whatever he wanted.

But the past bubbled up, and drove him to the drugs and alcohol; reconnected him to the life he'd left behind. Funny how the booze he despised as a child could do that.

The alcohol and drugs were a familiar escape, and he had the money to afford whatever he wanted. Heavy-duty mechanic; an honourable trade. He just didn't know how to deal with a past that haunted him.

Murder. Tears welled up at the memory of his mother. She was his rock. She'd never guessed he'd become a Clark Parker, or at least never brought it up. He liked to think she believed he was a good boy who listened to his mom. He should have been home. Maybe he could have stopped it from happening. His mom never deserved what his dad dished out. His mind floated back to the day he found his parents. It was the worst day of his life, and yet it was the turning point. He'd spent four glorious years with foster parents who cared. They straightened him out. Gave him a foundation.

It wasn't till after trade school and an influx of cash that he fell back into bad habits. Booze and drugs took away the second chance life had thrown at him.

A rap on the door pulled him from his head, and he glanced at the clock on the wall. *Shit.*

"Paul, you in there?" The door opened. "You know the rules. Out by 8:00."

Paul scrambled to his feet, slung his backpack over his shoulder and slipped his feet into sneakers worth more than his current bank account. "Yeah, sorry about that. Just dozed off. I'm out of here."

He swung past the hall monitor, an eighty-year-old man who volunteered at the shelter.

"Have a good day." Paul heard the old man mutter, but he didn't respond.

The Salvation Army shelter rules were strict. No drugs or alcohol, out by eight a.m. and back by eleven p.m.

Most days he wandered the streets, bumming cigarettes and money when he could. But today, he had other plans. He strode into the garage at the end of the street, pausing outside to straighten his hair in the window.

"What can I do you for?"

"Just wondering if you're looking for a mechanic. I've got heavy-duty mechanic experience and am looking for work." Paul rolled down his sleeves past his elbow, hoping he wasn't too late to hide the marks.

"Might just be your lucky day..."

CHAPTER THIRTY-ONE
May 15, 2018

It had been quite the day in court. Maybe April Somersby had it all figured out. Maybe he didn't need to make sure she found the card he tucked into her front-step mailbox that morning. But she hadn't brought up the other reason it may not be Paul Giovanni's blood at the scene. And that left too much doubt.

April Somersby descended the courthouse steps and battled her way through reporters to her car. He hoped she was heading home. He needed to see her retrieve the card and hoped she'd figure it out like he did and blow the prosecution's case wide open.

She climbed into the sports car and pulled out her phone to check messages. He exhaled slowly. Patience is what he needed more of most days. He was used to getting in, doing the job, and getting out. He was more involved than he wanted. Finally, her back-up lights came on and she maneuvered herself out of the parking stall. He waited till a car pulled in behind her, then followed at a safe distance. They ventured out onto the freeway and he could see April's red car out ahead. He floored the Honda Civic in an attempt to catch up and cursed under his breath the need for him to drive such a common gutless car. He kept his eyes on her in the distance, doing his best to keep her in his vision. She passed the exit to her office, which was a good sign. He lost sight of her, momentarily, but then saw her signal light ahead turn right. He slowed down and turned, following her lead. In front of him, April Somersby's little red sports car pulled to the side, and she inserted a key into a mail box in the super-box on the street corner.

"Shit." He lowered his eyes and looked out the left window. Hopefully, he hadn't caught her attention. He pulled over further down the block and watched in the rear-view mirror as she pulled into her garage, the door closing behind her.

He'd dropped the card into her mailbox at the front door that morning after she'd left for the courthouse. It hadn't occurred to him she might not even use that mailbox. Now what? She might not look in her mailbox for weeks.

After today in court, he thought maybe she already knew about the card. But she didn't press the expert witness, and it didn't appear she'd put it together, so she needed to find that card. If she didn't get it right, he had a lot to lose.

CHAPTER THIRTY-TWO
May 15, 2018

Paul waited in the visitor's meeting room. April said she'd come by in a couple of hours to discuss the next day's strategy. They had nothing to turn this around as far as he could see. He hoped April could convince him otherwise.

The door buzzed open and April marched in. She'd changed into jeans and a sweater and she was on a mission.

"Okay, Paul, let's get down to it. Is there any chance you have an identical twin walking around?" Paul noted she wore lipstick, and a faint waft of perfume emanated from the other side of the table.

"No, I don't think there's any chance. My mom never would have been able to give a child up for adoption. We were poor, and she lived under the rule of my drunken father, so maybe she had no choice? I wouldn't know where to start. Zoe has been through her DNA matches several times. No one else comes up as an unknown relative. If there was an identical twin, you think he, or his children, might show up." Paul leaned forward, turning his hands palms up. "Nothing."

April shook her head and exhaled. "We have to place you at the scene the day of the murder as you've told me and hope that creates doubt rather than supports a guilty verdict."

"I want to take the stand and tell my story. I'm innocent." Paul leaned back and met April's eyes. "I was sketchy about details at first, but those details are now my only hope."

"We have to prepare, but not tonight. You try to get some sleep as will I. Tomorrow I'll put our DNA expert on the stand, then after court, we'll prepare you for the questions the prosecution might ask."

"We've already been through this? Do I really need another go through?" Paul knew the answer before April delivered it.

"Listen, this is your life. One more go through. One more polish. I wouldn't be doing my job if I didn't do it." April stood to leave, then paused.

"Don't give up Paul. Today was a good day in court. We have a chance here."

Paul stared at the floor. She probably gave that speech to all her clients. But if she didn't believe there was a chance, she couldn't do her job. Thankfully, she seemed determined to fight for him.

*****

April buzzed out of the prison into the calming rays of a

setting sun, washing away her feelings of guilt. Taking an evening off was a luxury, and David promised her a quick dinner out. He was picking her up in twenty minutes. She was glad she'd changed before going to see Paul.

She drove into the garage just as David pulled up. She held up her hand to him and closed the garage door before setting her briefcase inside the kitchen entrance and exiting out the front door.

David leaned on the passenger door of his car with his sunglasses tucked in the front of his black tight-fitting t-shirt.

"There's the lady of the hour. I heard the news on the way over. Sounds like you had a good day in court."

April strode up and placed a hand on his chest before leaning in for a kiss. She pulled away and looked into his eyes. "Not as good as it could've been. I created some doubt and made the jurors pay attention, but at this point, the case is weak."

David opened the door and she slid into the passenger seat. He closed her door before rounding the vehicle and taking his place behind the wheel.

"From what I heard; the media liked what you did today. No matter the outcome of this case, you have a bright career, Ms. Somersby. Now let's go for a quick dinner, then get you home for a good sleep before tomorrow. Tell me you don't have to do any more work tonight?"

April looked at him sideways. "No, but I don't need any distractions, either."

David grinned and took his hand off the wheel and saluted. "Promise. Scouts honour."

"Instead of waiting on a table and then dinner, why don't we pick up fish and chips and head down to Stanley Park?"

"Your wish is my command." David reached over and squeezed her hand.

*****

April strolled up the front sidewalk. David insisted on walking her to her door, even though he knew he wouldn't be coming in tonight. She pulled the keys out of her purse and fumbled with the lock. It wasn't often she went through her front door. The thought of the unlocked door from a few weeks before reminded her she needed to use it more often.

"Looks like you've got a few flyers here." David reached in and pulled out yellowed flyers from the mailbox.

"Seems people can't read the sticker that says no flyers. I don't even bother pulling them out anymore until they spill over." Thanks. She turned from the open doorway to take the flyers, only to find David bent over, picking something up off the ground.

"This hit my foot when I pulled the flyers out." He handed her a white plastic card.

April's eyebrows knit and she tried to read what was on it, but the outdoor light above the step was off. "Thanks. Can't imagine what that is." She took the flyers from his other hand and placed them on the entryway table before returning to the open doorway. "Thank you for a lovely dinner. It's just what I needed."

David bent over and their lips met in a long, passionate kiss. He pulled away and cleared his throat. "Okay, Ms. Somersby. You have a big day tomorrow. Don't stay up too late."

Even in the dim light, April saw his wink. For something that once irritated her so much, she realized she was becoming fond of it.

CHAPTER THIRTY-THREE
May 16, 2018

He waited outside the courthouse for April Somersby to show. Every other day he entered the courtroom after her, but today she hadn't yet appeared. He thought perhaps she'd caught a ride with someone else. Her car was nowhere to be seen.

His fingers thrummed the steering wheel. *Where the hell was she?*

He stepped out of the car and scanned the parking lot. No red Lexus. He sprinted across the street and up the stairs to the courthouse. Removing his wallet and keys as he entered and placing them in the security bins. He grabbed them on the other side of the x-ray machines and sprinted down the hall, glancing at his watch. *She must have arrived earlier with someone else.* He pulled his ball cap down, put on the thick-rimmed glasses with clear glass lenses, and opened the door to courtroom 101 just a crack. He peered down the centre aisle. April Somersby's chair remained empty. He walked down the aisle, glancing from side to side, praying for an empty space. At last, he noticed one too close to the front for his comfort, but better than missing out on the proceedings. He pointed to the person sitting next to the empty spot. "Empty?" The woman nodded and everyone tucked in their feet to accommodate him.

He glanced at the front of the room again and pushed on toward the one remaining space left in the courtroom to sit.

He sat straight, focusing on the front of the room. Nora's salt and pepper hair and Zoe's long, dark waves sat a few feet in front of him. Beyond them, Paul came into view. He faced the gallery and their eyes met. *Shit.* He glanced down quickly and slouched in his seat. Had Paul recognized him? He wiped the beads of sweat from his forehead and slouched down to blend into the crowd.

The volume in the courtroom increased as the back door swung open and April Somersby breezed in, the click of her heels on the marble floor distinctive above the murmurs. Her ponytail bobbed at the back of her head. He slouched down more, anticipating Paul might call attention to him. But he could see April Somersby digging in her briefcase and flipping through papers.

He breathed a sigh of relief and sat up before standing as the judge entered.

Come on, April Somersby. Do your job. Get Paul off so I can get out of this shithole of a town.

CHAPTER THIRTY-FOUR
May 16, 2018

Paul scanned the courtroom. It was a full house. April's work the other day caused a stir. An open and shut case now had a hint of doubt. Everyone wondered if April would pull a twin out of thin air.

And Joe? He was thankful Joe didn't know about his connection to Lori Trembley, or if he did, he kept it to himself.

Paul's gaze rested on someone he recognized as they entered the courtroom. Was that the man who visited him in jail, Sam White? He scanned the benches, hesitating at the back, then moving forward till he found a seat about three rows behind Nora and Zoe. Their eyes met, and Sam bowed his head. *It was him.* Those eyes looked so familiar, but why? What the hell was he doing here? Paul's heart raced. He glanced at Nora, who knit her brows, a questioning look in her eyes. He smiled weakly in her direction and turned back around.

Where was April? It wasn't like her to be late. He wanted to point Sam out to her before he left. He watched the clock behind the judge's bench. Five minutes till court would be called into session.

He scanned the jurors. They didn't seem as hostile to him today. The one who always stared at him had the hint of a smile. His knee bounced up and down. He stilled it.

Damn it April. Where are you? This won't look good.

He felt the rush of air as the door at the back of the courtroom opened and April whirled in to take the seat beside him. Dishevelled like he'd never seen her before.

He cocked his head and leaned in to tell her about Sam White sitting behind them, but she held up her hand and opened a file folder. He leaned back in his chair and sighed. Her hair was pulled back in a ponytail, and she wasn't wearing earrings. He didn't think he'd ever seen her without earrings. Her eyes appeared sunken, and she had a frantic air about her as she shuffled through the papers in front of her.

Anger rose in his throat. For whatever reason, he'd woken up ready to fight this morning. He just didn't know it would be his lawyer he'd be directing his anger to. She was unprepared on the first day they were to present witnesses? Had he made a mistake hiring her? She'd seemed distracted when she visited him after court the day before. Was she giving up on the case? Did she have something bigger in the works? Perhaps his case was merely a stepping stone for notoriety.

He glanced at the jurors. They all watched her. What was it she'd told him about making a good impression?

He felt the heat rise in his cheeks, and he swallowed the anger building in his throat. He stared at the table and placed his right hand on his knee to still it. Then clasped his hands in his lap. His jaw worked back and forth, causing a headache to radiate from his temples.

Paul glanced back. He could only see the top of Sam White's head a few rows back. He reached across and touched April's arm, hoping she'd let him talk. She glared back at him. He removed his hand and cleared his throat before taking a deep breath. Something definitely wasn't right.

*****

April's heart pounded in her chest, and the air in her lungs burned. She placed her hands on the table to steady herself, taking a moment to inhale and slow her heart and breathing.

She sat down and fished around in her bag, pulling out files and the plastic card she'd stowed in the side pocket.

April straightened the papers in her folder and turned to Paul, who muttered something before she cut him off. "Is this your donor card?"

Paul's eyes narrowed, and he grabbed the card, turning it over twice before nodding his head.

"Did you have someone put it in my mailbox?"

Paul's eyebrows furrowed before shaking his head. "What's going on?"

"I'm not sure. I was up all night trying to figure out why someone would leave your donor card in my mailbox.

The courtroom quieted, and the bailiff announced the judge's arrival. April pushed back her chair and rose to her feet while staring into Paul's eyes. "Have you ever donated bone marrow?"

Paul nodded in response as they settled back into their chairs.

April's breath caught in her throat, and a slow grin spread across her face. She patted Paul's hand and turned her attention to the front of the room.

"Ms. Somersby, are you ready to call witnesses?" The judge's voice carried an edge of annoyance. Or was it boredom? April needed to be on cue today of all days.

"Your Honour, I'd like to call my first witness, Dr. Jan Whitmore."

A woman rose from the gallery. Her polyester suit jacket bulged around the button fastened at the front and the sound of fabric on fabric sliced through the air as she made her way to the front of the room. She placed her hand on the bible and agreed to tell the truth before settling into the witness stand.

"Dr. Whitmore, can you please tell the court a little about yourself as it pertains to your presence here today as an expert in molecular diagnostics?"

Dr. Whitmore cleared her throat, glancing at Paul before returning her gaze to April. "I've been working in molecular diagnostics for the past twenty years. I hold two PhDs in the field, one specializing in paternal DNA testing and one in forensic testing."

The air in the room hung thick with anticipation. A DNA match left little room for doubt, unless April could pull a twin out of thin air.

"Have you analyzed the DNA results presented by the prosecution?" April strode toward the bench. Her heart beat quickly, but her voice resonated calm and measured.

"Yes, I have."

"And do you arrive at the same conclusion as the expert witness provided by the prosecution? Do the DNA results match?"

"Yes, I do. The two results carry the same DNA."

April turned to the jury and smiled. "I'm glad you put it that way, Dr. Whitmore. It's the same DNA, but that doesn't mean it's from the same person, now does it."

Dr. Whitmore shifted in her seat and hesitated. "No, not necessarily, but likely."

"But not one hundred per cent guaranteed. Am I right?"

"Yes. They could belong to an identical twin."

"Is there anyone other than an identical twin who may carry identical DNA?"

Silence fell on the courtroom. But before the doctor could respond, April continued. "Dr. Whitmore, is it possible for someone who's received a bone marrow transplant to carry the donor's DNA?"

Dr. Whitmore's face lit up, and she nodded. "Yes, yes it is."

April turned to the jury. "And can you please explain how that can happen?"

April extended her hand in the jury's direction, and Dr. Whitmore took her cue, focusing her attention on the jury; speaking directly to them.

"While the science is new, studies have shown that sometimes bone marrow from the donor produces immune cells that take over several tissues of the recipient. The recipient becomes a chimera. Which means blood and some other tissues will contain the DNA of the donor, while others retain the recipient's own DNA. There's been cases reported where the recipient carried the donor DNA in several of their bodily fluids and tissues, while retaining their own DNA in others."

"So, Dr. Whitmore, if Paul Giovanni donated bone marrow, could it be possible the recipient carries the same DNA?"

"Yes. Yes, it is possible."

April turned toward the gallery. Paul sat at the defence table, eyes wide and face as pale as the white shirt he wore under his suit jacket.

*****

The courtroom erupted and the judge's gavel called for order while the prosecution team huddled in discussion.

April's heels punctuated the air like exclamation points as she returned to the defence table and retrieved the plastic card she'd left in full view.

Paul grabbed her arm and pulled her close. "I had no idea."

April patted his hand and returned to the front of the room, holding the card up before the jury. "Your Honour, I'd like to present into evidence the donor card of Paul Giovanni."

The courtroom erupted. April glanced back at Paul. He peered over his shoulder, studying the back of the gallery as if searching for someone.

The prosecutor leaped to his feet. "Your Honour, this is courtroom theatrics. Why wasn't this evidence presented earlier?"

"Your Honour, I just became aware of this piece of evidence last night. My client didn't even know I had it until I walked in here this morning. I would like to request a recess until next Wednesday to give me time to further explore the details of the bone marrow transplant.

April held her breath. She needed the recess to pull her case together.

"Quiet in the courtroom." The judge scanned the gallery, and the frenzy died down. "I will grant you recess until Tuesday. Court dismissed."

April leaned over the witness stand and thanked Dr. Whitmore before rushing back to Paul. Nora and Zoe were already at the table, and she could hear Nora's voice above the ruckus.

"I didn't know you donated bone marrow? When? Why didn't you tell me? Why didn't you think this was important?" The anger and frustration in Nora's voice carried across the room.

April placed a hand on Nora's shoulder. "This isn't the time or the place to discuss this." She glanced at the prosecution who were on their feet, staring at Nora. "Walk with me, Nora and Zoe. Paul, I'll be over at the detention centre in half an hour. Think about dates and details of that bone marrow donation. I'll need all the details to put this together by Tuesday."

Paul grabbed April's arm as he scanned the courtroom behind him. "Sam White was here. That's what I was trying to tell you when you first sat down." He put a hand over his eyes to shield them from the courtroom lights. "But I don't see him now." Then his hand dropped to his side, and he turned to April. "I remember why he looked familiar to me."

April glanced at Paul. "That's great. Right now, we have more important things to deal with." She motioned for Nora and Zoe to follow her. "I'll be over to talk to you within the hour." She tossed a glance over her shoulder, noting Paul continuing to scan the gallery. As she stepped into the foyer, camera lights and microphones inundated her space. Nora and Zoe sunk back.

Susan Ormsby from CBC pushed a microphone in her face. "How'd you find out about the bone marrow donation?"

April hesitated. "I have no comments." April glanced back and reached for Nora's hand, pulling her through the media throng. She walked them to their car and explained as much as she could.

"The card just showed up in my mailbox. Do either of you know anything about it?"

Nora glanced around before speaking. "That card was in the shoebox where I found the newspaper clipping about Lori

Trembley's death. But I swear I left it in the box. I thought little of it. It's just a donor card. Everybody has a donor card. What made you think it had anything to do with a bone marrow transplant?"

"It was just a hunch on my part. I knew there had to be a reason someone left it in my mailbox, so I googled who gets a donor card and what types of blood donations people make. I then investigated what type of donation might cause someone to replicate the DNA of the donor. Bone marrow donor came up right away. I asked Paul before I called my witness if he was ever a bone marrow donor and he said yes. After that, I just prayed our expert witness would corroborate what I learned last night."

"But who put it in your mailbox? And how did they get it?" Nora studied the throng of people gathered outside the courthouse.

"I don't know Nora. But they're on Paul's side. If you don't feel comfortable going home, perhaps you could stay in a hotel tonight?"

Nora nodded, then turned to Zoe. "It wasn't you, was it?"

"Mom! No. I didn't even know about the shoebox. And if I had found it, the card wouldn't have meant anything to me."

Nora inhaled deeply. "Of course, honey. I'm just at my wit's end."

"Ladies, if you don't mind. I need to get to the detention centre, and track down the evidence needed to prove Paul donated bone marrow."

April gave Nora a hug and patted Zoe on the shoulder.

"Take care and be safe. Think about staying in a hotel, will you?"

Nora nodded again, and April marched off to her car, ponytail swinging from side to side.

CHAPTER THIRTY-FIVE
May 16, 2018

Paul perched on his chair in the visitation room, eyes glued to the door. He'd gone straight there from the courtroom to wait for April. *Sam White my ass.* Why hadn't he recognized him? It all made sense now. Or did it? The name Sam White clearly wasn't his real name. Paul knew him as John Smith. Why would John be trying to help him get off if he'd killed Lori Trembley?

He'd thought about nothing else than the bone marrow donation after he left the courtroom. It had been the early 80s. He'd just obtained his heavy-duty mechanic's ticket. They were the golden years, and he was still close to his foster parents. In fact, it was his foster mom who convinced him to donate blood and check off the willing to donate bone marrow option. She was such a positive influence in his life.

She'd arranged for him to meet John after the donation. The meeting was awkward, and they didn't seem to have much in common. John was a little younger and hardly said a word when they met. He refused to shake hands, citing he didn't like germs. Which, in hindsight, having battled leukaemia, the germ thing made sense. But he also kept folding the edge of the tablecloth over and over, seeming to get irritated it wouldn't fold perfectly. The meeting was short and Paul was glad when John didn't reach out. The duty was done. John thanked him for saving his life, and it pleased his foster mom that they met.

April breezed into the room and pulled Paul from his thoughts. She spoke before she even sat down. "Okay, Paul, we have to be open about this. When did you donate your bone marrow? Was it only once?"

Paul leaned forward. "It was only once, and it was the early 80s. I think 1982?"

"Why'd you do it? Was it to help someone you knew?"

"No, no, not at all. I'd donated blood and checked off that I'd be willing to be a bone marrow donor. They called about a year later saying I was a match for someone and would I come in for further testing. When I went in, further tests confirmed my compatibility to the person seeking a bone marrow donation."

April tapped the table impatiently. "And who was the recipient?"

"His name was John Smith. My foster mom arranged a meeting, but I only met with him once. He was about my age, maybe a little younger, and had leukaemia. A bone marrow transplant was his only hope."

"So, what did he look like?" April shook her head in

disbelief. "Don't take this wrong, but getting information out of you has been painful. Forgive me if I wonder what else you're not telling me."

Paul raised his hand. "I tried telling you in the courtroom that he was there. In the gallery."

"What?"

"Sam White. When he visited me in jail, there was something about him that looked familiar. When Dr. Whitmore said a bone marrow recipient could take on the DNA of the donor, I realized Sam White is John Smith."

April developed the ashen hue of the cement walls surrounding them. "Oh my God. Why would he risk that?"

"I have no idea. I've been asking myself the same thing. Why would he want to help me?"

April sat in silence, then sprang into action, colour returning to her cheeks. "Okay. I've petitioned the judge to have the files opened to identify the recipient. We'll need all that paperwork to corroborate your donation and name of the recipient, anyway. I'll also ask for close circuit footage at the courthouse to see if they captured him on camera. What did he look like?"

"He wore glasses with thick dark rims, a ball cap low over his face, and a grey jacket, I think. I didn't get a good look at him in the courtroom. When we met in jail, he had dark, curly hair.

Paul shook his head. "If I hadn't given John my bone marrow, he wouldn't have been alive to kill Lori Trembley." Paul slouched in his seat, leaning forward into his hands and resting his elbows on the table.

April rose from her chair. "Paul, try not to dwell on it. I've got to get going. If we're lucky, we'll get access to those records today and get a clear image of John Smith. Otherwise, we'll be waiting until after the weekend."

April strode through the door, and Paul sat for a few minutes. A shiver ran up his spine. *How did John know Lori, and what reason did he have for killing her? Did he donate his bone marrow to a contract killer?*

*****

Paul waited anxiously. No word from her since she visited him last Wednesday. Monday at noon, he requested a call to his attorney.

"April, what's going on? Did you get the petition?" Paul stood in the visitor's room, with the wall phone receiver to his ear.

"Sorry, Paul, the petition just came through. I'm on my way to the Canadian Blood Services main office with the subpoena. We found the guy you described on the closed-circuit footage from the courthouse, but we couldn't see his face. He knew how to keep it concealed from the cameras. I promise I'll call you back when I have something to report."

Paul hung up the phone and sighed.

*****

On Tuesday, April strode into the visitation room with a folder in her hand, but she didn't appear hopeful. "Well, we have confirmed you donated bone marrow to John Smith on May 2, 1982. He was five years younger than you.

Paul raised his eyebrows. He was sure they were closer in age than that.

"He lived in Vancouver with his parents, Ed and Marg. No siblings. Ed and Marg are no longer alive. Died in a plane crash in 1990. It's like John Smith disappeared after that. He has an aunt who's still alive. I called her, and she said after the funeral, no one ever heard from John again."

Paul threw his hands in the air. "Well, that's great. What can he want?"

"Listen Paul, it'd be better if we could deliver a warm body matching the DNA found at the scene. Hopefully, he'll show up at the courthouse again and we can arrest him. What did he look like when you met him after the donation? We have the CC footage of when he visited you here, but again, he kept his face hidden from the cameras."

"Back in the day, he was blonde, tall, well built. Other than blue eyes, the man who visited me here wasn't the same man at all."

"So, do you think he was wearing a disguise when he visited you here?"

"Without a doubt. It was gutsy, that's for sure. He counted on me not recognizing him."

"When we get back into court tomorrow, I'll put you on the witness stand to create a larger wedge of doubt in the juror's minds. I worry that the coincidence of a man you donated marrow to, killing the woman you had contact with the day of the murder, may be too much to overcome for some of them. It's important the jurors humanize you so they understand the gravity of their decision."

Paul nodded and swallowed the lump in his throat. If they found John Smith, Paul worried about what else they might learn. They didn't need a warm body, just enough doubt to get him off.

CHAPTER THIRTY-SIX
May 22, 2018

April rose and straightened her skirt before approaching the witness stand. "Paul, tell me what you were doing in the early 1970s." She stared into his eyes, encouraging him to respond just like they practiced.

Paul cleared his throat and stared past April toward Nora and Zoe. The pause was long.

Come on Paul. Do it like we practiced. Long pauses give the jurors time to doubt your answers.

Paul's eyes returned to hers, and he straightened in his chair. "I was a member of the Clark Park Gang."

"And how old were you?"

"Twelve."

April waited for him to continue, but he stared blankly back at her.

"And why did you join a gang in the 1970s?" April took a step back. The courtroom waited in silence.

"I was an only child with an alcoholic, abusive father and a mother who worked too hard. We lived in East Van. When I went anywhere, I was a sitting duck. The gangs picked on a loner. If I didn't join a gang, I was going to get beat up."

"And you did get beat up, didn't you?"

"Yes, before I joined the Clark Parkers, a few of the Riley Park members roughed me up for wandering into their territory one day. That's when I realized I needed a gang behind me for protection."

"And did you know Lori Trembley in those days?"

Again, Paul turned his gaze to Nora and Zoe. April turned to look at them. Their facial expressions remained neutral, just like she'd coached them. Nora even gave a small nod of encouragement to him.

"Yes, I did. She was the sister of a Riley Park member. No one knew about us. We'd meet in neutral territory and talk. Nothing serious, just teenage kid stuff. Neither of us wanted to be involved in gangs, but had no other choice."

"Did you keep in touch after you left the gang?"

"We stayed in touch for a couple years, but we met less frequently and her life changed when her brothers joined another gang and she got sucked in as well. Eventually, we lost touch."

"And it was during this time that you donated your bone marrow?"

"Yeah. My foster mom encouraged me to donate blood and sign up as a bone marrow donor. She had a friend with a child that needed a bone marrow donation. I didn't match for the friend's daughter, but I got a call to undergo further testing as I was a preliminary match for someone in their database. Turns out I matched, and so I donated."

"Did you know the recipient?"

"No. Not at the time. But not long after I donated, we met up. He also lived in Vancouver and needed the transplant because he had leukemia. He thanked me for the donation."

"Did you ever meet up again?"

"No, the two of us didn't have much in common. He was quiet and we never hit it off at that meeting. And I just graduated from trade school and landed a good job. I never thought much about him until you brought the donation up the other day."

April strode back to the defence table and picked up the documents she'd retrieved from Canadian Blood Services. "Your Honour, I submit into evidence the paperwork verifying Paul Giovanni's bone marrow donation on May 2, 1982 to a Mr. John Smith."

April turned to the gallery and saw the courtroom door swing closed. She turned to Paul, who stared at the floor, struggling to keep his emotions in check.

"Okay, Paul, so you got on with your life. What did that look like?"

"Well, at first it was great. I got my heavy-duty mechanics ticket and landed a great job in the oilfield in Alberta. They'd fly me in for three weeks and out for one. I made obscene amounts of money for someone in their twenties. So much disposable income that I spent foolishly. Cars, women…" Paul halted as he glanced in Nora's direction again. "And drugs."

"Did you join another gang?"

"No. I knew better. I wanted nothing to do with gang life."

"And did you reconnect with Lori Trembley?"

"Yes. Now that I was partying and finding myself in bar fights, our paths crossed one evening and we reconnected."

"Was it a romantic relationship?"

"No. There was never any romance. We were good friends, and I stayed over a time or two, but there was never any long-term commitment. In fact, we kept our visits quiet, as we didn't know how her brothers would react or the new gang members she was associated with."

"What gang was she with?"

"The Big Circle Boys."

"When was the last time you saw Lori?"

"The day she died."

The gallery burst into chatter.

"Order, I'll have order in my courtroom." Judge Munroe

glared at the gallery, and the din subsided.

April took the break to face the jury and assess the damage. Three jurors scowled, and the rest remained devoid of emotion.

When the room quietened, April faced Paul and continued. "What happened that day?"

Paul took a deep breath, this time avoiding any glances at Nora and Zoe. "The night before Lori died, I'd gotten into a brawl at a pub and some guy knifed me. I should have gone to a hospital, but I was afraid of the questions they'd ask, and didn't want to confront the police, so I went to Lori's apartment. She cleaned and bandaged me up, even put a couple of stitches in. She had experience with tending to the wounds of her brothers. The wound was shallow. I left about noon the next day and went home, where I slept off the bender. The next morning when I woke, I saw the news and learned of Lori's murder." Paul's voice trailed off and his head bent forward.

"When you left Lori Trembley, she was alive and well?"

Paul scanned the jurors. Would they believe him? "Yes. She lectured me about how I needed to get my life back on track. The last words she said to me were 'Paul, you're…'" The words caught in his throat. He paused, then continued. "'better than this.'" He wiped a hand across his eyes and cleared his throat. When I saw her picture on the news the next morning, I emptied my bottles of booze and dumped my cocaine down the toilet. Her last words have echoed in my head every day since. Her words put me on the path to sobriety and my wife Nora has kept me there"

Paul glanced at Nora before lowering his eyes to his black

leather shoes. He prayed his face didn't give away what else happened before he left Lori Trembley that morning.

"Why didn't you go to the police when you learned of Lori's death on the news the next day?"

Paul raised his gaze back to the jury, just as April had instructed him to do. "I was scared. Scared they'd blame me and scared her brothers would assume I'd done the shooting and get to me before I could prove my innocence. I knew I hadn't killed her and I didn't have any idea who did. There was no reason to come forward. There was nothing I could do to help the police solve the case."

The jurors stared back at Paul. All seemed enthralled with his words, but not all appeared empathetic.

"One more thing, Paul. Have you ever fired a gun?"

"Never. I've never owned or even held a gun. The Clark Parkers didn't carry guns, so even in my gang days I wasn't around guns."

"I have no further questions, your Honour."

*****

The prosecution approached Paul, with a grin from ear to ear.

"So, Mr. Giovanni, you knew Lori Trembley?"

April jumped to her feet. "Objection, your Honour. I think we've established that."

"Sustained." The judge turned to the prosecution. "Keep it

relevant, please."

The prosecution turned back to Paul. "When you say your relationship with Lori Trembley wasn't romantic, does that mean you never slept with her?"

Paul squirmed in his seat. April said he'd ask this, and to keep his answer short. "No."

"Meaning you slept with her?"

"Yes."

"And was it a tumultuous relationship? Did you fight a lot?"

"No. We were good friends. We just knew we couldn't have a long-term relationship. Her brothers would've killed me."

"So, instead you killed her?"

"NO! I cared for her. I would never hurt her."

"You would just have us believe you were in her apartment the day of her murder, and that your doppelgänger bone marrow recipient swooped in and killed her?"

"I can't explain who killed her or why. I just know it wasn't me."

"Rather convenient. You say you were at the end of a two-day bender when you visited Lori's apartment. And yet you seem to remember things clearly. How can that be?"

Paul glanced at April. They'd rehearsed this question too. "I can't say I remember everything, but I remember the pain from the wound, Lori stitching me up and then leaving around noon the next day, as she was expecting her brothers to stop by that afternoon. I took a bus home. The next thing I remember is waking with a splitting headache the following morning and sitting in front of the TV with a coffee when Lori's face flashed across the screen."

"And it didn't occur to you to come forward? Tell the police what you knew?"

"As I explained it wouldn't have helped the police and Lori's brothers or fellow gang members would taken justice into their own hands and have killed me too. Instead, I vowed to do what Lori told me. Get clean and lead a good life. And that's what I've done."

"I understand two people attacked you in jail. Is that correct?"

Paul shot April a quick glance. "Yes."

"And who were your attackers?"

"I believe it was a couple of former Riley Park gang members."

"Why would they attack you?"

Paul sat up straight and glared at the prosecutor. "Oh, I don't know. Perhaps because I'm accused of Lori Trembley's murder, and they're pissed about it?"

Paul didn't look at April. He knew she'd be shooting him warning glances. He'd tried to remain calm, but that was just a stupid question.

"Or maybe they know you killed Lori Trembley?"

April rose from her seat. "Speculation, your Honour. Move to strike."

"Prosecution, watch your questioning. Sustained."

"No more questions, your Honour."

The prosecutor strode back to his table, and Paul glared after him. He'd made his point, and even though the objection was sustained, the impression he wanted to make was left with the jurors.

HEATHER GRAY

CHAPTER THIRTY-SEVEN
May 22, 2018

He sat in his car outside the courthouse, dialed his handler's number and waited for a connection.

"What is it?"

No hello. No, what news is there? Just get to the point. The man cleared his throat. "I just left the courthouse. The defence has presented an excellent case explaining why Paul's DNA wasn't at the scene. It'll be all over the news shortly if it isn't already, but I wanted you to hear it from me."

"Stop with the intrigue. What's the scoop?"

"Turns out Paul and I share the same DNA."

"Sounds pretty far-fetched to me."

The man heard typing on a keyboard. *He can't even give me a minute of his undivided attention.*

"Look, when I was a teenager, I had a condition where I needed a bone marrow transplant. I matched to someone. Turns out that someone was Paul Giovanni. As an expert witness testified today, recipients of bone marrow donors can produce the donor's DNA in some tissues and not others. It would explain why the DNA tested on my blood at the scene matched Paul Giovanni's and why the hair didn't match to him."

The typing on the other end of the phone paused. "Well, I'll be damned. Looks like I might owe you an apology."

The man grinned. "So, can I get a plane to come pick me up tonight?"

"Not so fast. Didn't you tell me Paul Giovanni knew Lori Trembley? Seems like a pretty big coincidence that you, being a marrow donor from Giovanni, would be the executioner. Is there more you need to tell me?"

"Honestly, I can't believe it either. But I may as well also tell you that on the stand it also came out today that Paul was in Lori's apartment the morning, I killed her."

Silence flooded the connection. "You realize the client will never believe this? Unless Paul Giovanni goes free, you'll be looking for a new career. And you'll never work in this industry again."

"So, I guess I won't be waiting for a plane this evening?"

"You guessed right. Sounds like you had a partner you forgot to tell anyone about. The client won't be pleased when this hits the news."

The line went dead, and the man leaned his head against the headrest.

CHAPTER THIRTY-EIGHT
May 22, 2018

"I walked into the house after getting groceries that day and paused. I don't know why. The house just seemed different. But nothing was out of place. There was no reason to feel that way, although now I know there was." Nora's voice caught, and she raised her hand to her mouth.

Paul reached across the space between them, stopping before he touched her. "Clearly someone was in the house, but we don't know exactly when. I'm just glad you weren't home when they were there. Are you sure nothing was out of place?"

Nora raised her eyes to meet his. "Nothing. But Paul, they were in our bedroom!" She stopped short and bowed her head, swallowing the words.

"Well, it was likely John Smith. It appears he's trying to help us."

"True, but the fact he got into our house and out again without me knowing makes me very anxious." Nora's eyes brimmed with tears.

"Oh honey, I'm so sorry. Maybe you and Zoe should go stay at a hotel?"

"We've been staying with my mom, Paul. I can't go back home until you're there with me."

"But Nora, what if that never happens?"

"Surely a jury will have reasonable doubt. They can't convict you if there's doubt."

"That's certainly my hope."

A long pause followed before Nora raised her eyes to his. "What do you know about John Smith?"

Paul shifted in his seat, avoiding eye contact with Nora. "He's visited me here."

"What? Why didn't you say something?" Nora's anger caught the guard's attention, and he stepped closer.

"I didn't know, Nora. I didn't recognize him. It was only when April brought up the bone marrow donation, I realized who'd visited me."

"So, a hit man visited you in jail, and was likely in our house? Doesn't this concern you?"

"But he's trying to help us. I don't think he's any threat to you, Zoe, or me. He wants to get me off the charge."

"But Paul, it makes no sense. Why would he want to get you off and have people looking for him?"

"I don't know. Maybe it's his way of paying me back for the donation? It's the only reason I can think of."

Nora wiped her eyes with the back of her hand and cleared her throat before rising. "I promised to take Mom to a doctor's appointment."

"I'm so sorry, Nora."

She glanced at him, smiling weakly before being escorted from the room.

Paul remained sitting with his elbows on the table, head in his hands.

Only one shameful secret left to keep buried.

HEATHER GRAY

CHAPTER THIRTY-NINE
May 22, 2018

"Jesus!" April jumped at the sound of her doorbell. She'd lost herself in the evidence and closing remarks. She needed to get this just right. *It better not be some religious zealot standing at my door.*

She peeked out of the living room window. David stood waiting with a bag of takeout food in his hand. She didn't have time for distractions, but she had to admit she was happy to see him. Glancing in the mirror on her way to the front door, she noticed the black rings under her eyes. She sighed as she released the deadbolt and turned the doorknob.

"Hello beautiful. Surprise!"

April grinned and motioned him inside. "Well, how can I turn anyone away with that kind of greeting?"

David closed the door behind him, before lifting her chin as he leaned into a passionate kiss. April didn't resist, even though her head told her to send him away.

"You don't mind, do you?" David took a step back and stared into her eyes.

"I mind a lot. You're a distraction, David Windsor."

"Why thank you, April Somersby. I promise I won't stay long, but once again I felt the need to feed you. You can't go without food. You have a big day tomorrow. When you win this thing, you'll be the most sought-after defence attorney in Vancouver.

April grinned up at him. "As long as you don't run from the attention, I'll be a happy woman."

David grinned before walking into the kitchen. He unpacked the food on the island. "Shall we?"

"It smells delicious." April brushed past him as she reached into the cupboard and pulled down two plates. They settled in at the island beside each other.

"So, how are the closing statements coming?"

April sighed. "Slow. Is a handful of hair and a bone marrow donation enough doubt?"

David grinned. "That would be the million-dollar question. Want to run what you have by me?"

"No, I'm not quite at that point yet."

"It's too bad those hairs didn't turn up an identity. That would make it an open-and-closed case, I would assume?"

"It would certainly help. But I keep reminding myself I'm not here to convict someone else. I just need to provide enough reason for doubt. The one thing I know the jury will question is that Paul and his bone marrow recipient were both in Lori Trembley's apartment the day of her murder. Even I have trouble with that one. I just can't figure it out. Coincidences like this just don't happen in real life. It's a neatly wrapped package with a bow. A gift. I don't know how the jury will deal with it."

David remained quiet as he finished his plate of food. He pushed the last grain of rice around on his plate, deep in thought. "Maybe you're overthinking it. The hair alone should provide doubt. The explanation for the blood at the site should be enough, don't you think? And can't you find the bone marrow recipient? You have a name, so you should be able to find him, right?"

"We're having trouble with that. It appears he disappeared into thin air in 1990. But Paul says he's seen the donor in the courtroom. He didn't recognize him at first, but apparently, he visited him in jail, too. He put two and two together when I pointed out the bone marrow donation in court."

David grabbed April's hand. "That's fantastic! You must have CC footage to help you identify him, then?"

"No, it appears our man is a master at avoiding cameras." April paused, stroking the back of David's hand with her thumb while raising her eyes to his. "But at this point, it doesn't matter who it is, just that there's someone else who is a legitimate suspect. Like I said, I'm not here to convict someone else. I'll leave the detective work to the police."

"And that's why you'll be the most sought-after lawyer in Vancouver." David rose and repackaged the leftovers before placing them in the fridge.

"Why don't you take those home?"

"No, I'll leave them for you." David's voice floated away as if he was about to say something else, but thought better of it.

"Sorry, but I really do have to get back to it." April placed a hand on his shoulder. He turned and held her close, his breathing stilted.

"Look, I can't wait for all of this to be over. We'll have a big celebration." David lifted her chin and stared into her eyes.

For the first time in their relationship, she noticed something in those eyes that disturbed her. Something dark. She shivered. Then his lips devoured hers and all thoughts of darkness slipped away.

CHAPTER FORTY
May 24, 1994

A mix of snow and rain pelted down, forming a thin sheet of ice. Black ice. Paul rounded a curve on the Sea to Sky Highway leading from Whistler back to Vancouver.

He drove to Whistler for the weekend, not to ski, although surprisingly the hill was still open late in May, but to spend some time thinking about his life and the way forward. His new job at the garage had allowed him this opportunity. Lori's death ate at him, and he knew he needed to deal with it. Was there anything he could have done to prevent it? Was her death because of him? The news casts reported predictions about what was going to happen now. They assumed it was a gang related murder.

As his Volkswagen rental successfully navigated the curve, he found himself face to face with a parking lot of twisted metal. Multiple cars involved in a tangled mess. Paul applied the brakes, and that's when he realized the extent of the black ice. He pushed the brake as hard as he could and held his breath, relying on the vehicle's onboard anti-skid system to take over. The car stayed on the road, coming to rest at an angle against a guardrail without hitting any of the cars in front of him. He threw the car into park and let out a long, slow breath.

Nothing like a brush with death to convince him that the plans he made in Whistler to detox and settle down were the right plans. He closed his eyes and thanked God for reminding him of what he really needed in life.

He didn't hear the car coming behind him as he unclipped his seatbelt. His head hit the windshield and the steering wheel dug into his ribs. He settled back into the seat, gasping for breath. *Why is there such a banging in my head?*

Before he could compute the sound, his driver's side door opened and a high-pitched voice filled the interior.

"Oh, my gosh. I'm so sorry. I couldn't stop. Thank God, I didn't push you through the guardrail." The voice paused, inhaling sharply. "Oh my God, are you okay?"

A petite blonde woman with a hand over her mouth stood beside him with tears pooling before spilling over.

"I'm okay. It's okay." Paul felt the need to reassure her. Then he realized the danger she was in as she stood on the highway. "Listen, climb into the backseat. If someone else comes around that corner and hits your car, you'll be in more danger out on the road than in the backseat of my car."

The woman nodded, closed his door and slid into the backseat. "I'm so sorry. How can I help you?"

Paul grimaced as he adjusted his rear-view mirror so he could see the woman breaking down in his backseat. Then flipped down the visor mirror to assess himself. Blood matted the hair on the top of his head. He winced as his abdomen brushed the steering wheel. Searing pain ripped through his chest and he forced himself to breathe shallowly. *Broken ribs.* He glanced back again.

"It's okay. I almost did the same to the car in front of me. You didn't hit hard. I took off the seatbelt before you hit. I'm surprised the airbag didn't deploy. You should buckle in. I can't with the pain in my chest, but you should. What's your name?"

"Nora. My name's Nora. Where's the pain in your chest? Is it your heart?"

"No, no. I think the steering wheel dug in on impact. Probably broken or bruised ribs. I've had those before."

"Is there anything I can get you? Snow off the side of the road to ice that injury?" Before Paul could protest, Nora scooted over to the other side of the car, opened the door, and scooped some snow off the side of the road. She packed it into a chip bag off the floor of the back seat. "Here." She pushed the icy package at him.

As he retrieved the bag from her, his fingers brushed hers and his breath caught, causing him to clear his throat. "Thanks Nora. I'm Paul. Looks like we'll be here for a while. Where you from? What do you do?"

Nora sat back in her seat, and the click of her seatbelt reassured him. He explored her large hazel eyes, staring back at him in the rear-view mirror.

"I'm from Vancouver and in my final year of Medical Laboratory Science at UBC."

The corners of her mouth turned up as he peered at her in the rear-view mirror. His head throbbed, and he wished he could put the ice on his head, but the stabbing pain when he lifted his arm told him otherwise. "Impressive. Sounds like a tough program. Nora, do you have a phone on you?"

"Yes, why?"

Paul whispered, "Dial 911" before he blacked out.

*****

Paul's eyes fluttered open, and he squinted to focus. A woman sat beside his bed holding his hand. He had time to study her before she noticed he'd woken up. Slight features, high cheekbones, blond hair swirling every which way. He glanced at her hand holding his. No ring. When he glanced back at her face, she dropped his hand.

"Sorry, I hope you don't mind. I mean they couldn't find a next of kin in your contacts on your phone, and I just felt so bad and was worried. Thought I'd sit with you till you woke up, at least."

"Mind? Of course not. But I'm afraid I'm not making the best first impression." He attempted a grin that turned to a grimace as pain shot through his chest and abdomen.

"Better than mine." Nora pursed her lips. "It's not usually how I 'hit' on guys."

Paul closed his eyes, unable to choke out a laugh. Her voice diminished as he fell back into a fitful sleep.

*****

The next time he woke, she was gone, and a nurse stood at the foot of his bed. "Welcome back."

"How long have I been out?"

"Only about four hours. Your friend left just a few minutes ago." The nurse checked his IV pole, punching in numbers and injecting something into the line.

"Did she say if she's coming back?" Paul didn't know why it mattered so much, but he wanted her beside his bed.

"She didn't say, but she left you a note on your nightstand."

Paul tried to reach across, but the pain in his side stopped him short.

"Here, let me get that for you. Do you want me to read it to you?"

"Sure," Paul stammered between the stabbing pains.

"Paul. I'll be back in the morning to check on you. Nora." The nurse paused. "Is she your girlfriend, wife, sister?"

"No, she's the woman who did this to me." Paul chuckled before succumbing to a fit of coughing that sent searing pain throughout his body.

"Oh really? Her concern made me think you must be related."

"She's way above my pay grade." Paul drifted off to sleep as the medication in the IV took hold.

CHAPTER FORTY-ONE
May 22, 2018

The man paced the corner balcony. Gazing toward the mountains for inspiration. Should he nudge April Somersby? Provide some of his hair to test against the hair at the crime scene? *Damn-it!* He needed her to find a match for his hair at the crime scene. Give the jury something tangible to hang on to and prove his presence at the crime scene to the client. It might create the deep-seated doubt that would result in a not-guilty verdict for Paul and re-establish trust with his client.

He strode into the apartment, stopping in the kitchen to first don rubber gloves, then grab a Ziploc bag from the cabinet drawer, before entering the ensuite bathroom. He stared at himself in the mirror. Was this the stupidest thing he'd ever done? He grabbed a few hairs and pulled, holding them up to the light to be sure they had the roots attached before placing them in the Ziploc. How much was enough? He grabbed a few more and pulled, placed them in the bag, and sealed it. With a black sharpie, he wrote April Somersby's name on the bag and signed his initials, J.S.

On the drive to the attorney's house, he wracked his brain about where to leave the evidence. Her office would be ideal, but he couldn't chance getting caught or seen on closed circuit footage, even with a disguise. He pulled up to her house, leaving the car running as he popped the bag into her front door mailbox. On the drive back to his hotel, he concluded he had no choice but to text April on a burner phone and instruct her to check her mailbox. He was running out of time.

CHAPTER FORTY-TWO
May 23, 2018

April approached the judge's bench, the prosecution trailing a few feet behind.

Paul glanced at the clock on the wall. Two minutes past ten. Today would have been closing statements, but April was asking for an extension. In light of additional evidence, she wanted 72 hours to present what might be his shining hope. Hair showed up in April's mailbox and it was out for testing. If it matched the hair at the scene, it would show John Smith was alive and well and at the scene of the murder. The jury would have to deliver a non-guilty verdict on account of reasonable doubt.

And yet, the judge and the prosecution were arguing about another delay. He turned around and met Nora's eyes. She smiled, trying to convey hope, but Paul's stomach turned.

"Court is adjourned."

Paul wheeled around in his chair to face the front.

"We'll see everyone back here in forty-eight hours."

Paul bowed his head and rubbed his eyes.

"Okay, Paul, I have to go. I don't know if forty-eight hours will be enough time, but I'll be demanding expedited DNA testing on that hair. I'll touch base when I can."

And with that, April Somersby marched out of the courtroom amid clicking cameras and shouts from reporters, asking questions she didn't answer.

Paul scoured the courtroom. No John Smith that he could see.

Paul waved at Nora, who waved back with a broad grin before the bailiff escorted him out of the courtroom.

Back in his cell, Paul paced. Where was John Smith? He'd given samples of his hair to April. He glanced at the clock on the wall. Nora and Zoe would be at his mother-in-law's by now. He needed to call them.

He pressed the button on the wall, calling for a guard.

Footsteps approached the door and Paul stood back. "Can I make a phone call, please?"

The guard leaned out the door, staring down the hall. "Sure. Looks like you can come right now."

Paul breathed a sigh of relief and stepped out of the cell.

He dialed the number and waited. Nora answered on the

second ring.

"Is everything okay? This is good news, isn't it? We wanted a recess."

"Everything's fine. Yes, it's good news. I just wanted to touch base with you. With the break-in last week, I'm worried. I know I said John Smith is on our side, but with his further involvement in the case, whether it's for my benefit or not, I'm more worried. I have an uneasy feeling and I want you and Zoe to be careful."

"We are Paul. Will forty-eight hours be enough time to get the testing done? I'm not even sure I understand why she's doing this. There should be enough doubt without having to show a match to the hair found in April's mailbox, don't you think?"

"I guess she just thinks it's better to have a little extra evidence. You never know how a jury's going to lean."

"I suppose. I just want you home and I want to go home. Seems like she's delaying your release."

"I know, honey. We'll get there. Just a few more days and I'll be home. But I'm getting the stink eye from the guard. I better go. Love you."

As Paul strode down the hallway to his cell, his fists flexed open and closed. *John Smith, what are you doing?*

CHAPTER FORTY-THREE
May 25, 2018

Two days later Paul shuffled alongside the bailiff as he led him to his chair at the defence table. April Somersby's chair sat empty beside him. Besides the one other day in court, she always arrived before him. Paul fidgeted, turning to glance back at the gallery behind him. Nora and Zoe spoke to each other in hushed tones. Paul scanned the courtroom for John Smith. No sign. He breathed a sigh of relief. People trickled in, trying to find an empty seat to occupy. But April was nowhere to be seen.

Paul glanced at the clock on the wall. Two minutes to one o'clock. *Come on April. Where are you?*

He hadn't heard from April, so assumed she still didn't have the DNA results. She hadn't convinced him that she needed them. Showing up without results would be better than not showing up at all. Paul quieted his bouncing leg and raised his eyes to the jury. No one talked to their neighbour. Each person settled into their space, likely hoping this would be the last day they'd have to sit in this courtroom.

Paul twisted to look back again. This time he saw a man at the back, head down, glancing side to side as he made his way down the aisle, settling in midway down the gallery on the opposite side of Nora and Zoe. He couldn't get a good look at him. Was it John Smith? Paul glanced back at Nora, who shot him a reassuring, but nervous, smile.

"Please rise."

Paul stood, glancing over his shoulder at the back of the courtroom once more. The doors remained closed. He cleared his throat quietly and waited for the judge to sit down behind her bench.

She raised her head after shuffling papers in front of her, first studying the prosecution bench, then resting her eyes on Paul and April's empty chair. She glanced up at the clock. Then stared back at Paul. "Mr. Giovanni, can you tell me why your lawyer isn't present?"

Paul pushed his chair back and stood. "I'm sorry your Honour, I don't know. I haven't heard from her." Paul remained on his feet.

Judge Monroe glanced toward the back of the courtroom before resting her gaze on Paul. She opened her mouth, then closed it again and shifted her concentration to the prosecution. "Have you by chance heard from Ms. Somersby?"

The prosecution rose as Paul sat back down. "No, your Honour. We have not."

The judge let out an audible sigh, glanced back at the clock, and thrummed her fingers on the dark oak bench top in front of her.

A rustling, and the sound of heels on the marble floor, broke the silence. Paul wheeled around to see a woman he didn't recognize, walk toward the front of the courtroom, open the gate between the front and the gallery, and slide into the chair beside Paul. She gave him a weak smile and reached up to smooth her shiny black hair.

"And who might you be?" The irritation in the judge's voice cut through the air and landed on the defence table.

The woman stood, straightening her grey pencil skirt as she did so. "Your Honour, my name is Donna Hall. I'm a junior lawyer in April's office. She's asked me to attend and ask for a delay of fifteen minutes in proceedings. She sends her apologies, but says she has the hair DNA results, and is on her way. The lab just finished the testing this past hour."

The prosecutor jumped to his feet. "Your Honour. You have already granted Ms. Somersby an extension. We ask that we proceed with closing statements."

The judge tapped her pen on the bench, its echoes reverberating around the courtroom as everyone awaited her pronouncement. "I understand your frustration. This is highly unusual and I don't take the request made by the defence lightly. At the same time, our goal is to ensure justice is served. I think we can wait another fifteen minutes. Let's reconvene at one-thirty." The deep, resonating bang of her gavel turned the silence to mayhem.

Paul turned to Donna. "Did she say what the DNA test found? Did the DNA match the hair at the crime scene?"

"I'm sorry, she didn't say. She was in a rush."

"How did her voice sound? Hopeful?"

"Panicked would be more like it. She knew she wouldn't make it on time."

Paul nodded. He turned again to search for John Smith in the gallery. People stood and milled about. The excitement in the room mirrored the volume of chatter. The seat where Paul thought he saw John Smith earlier sat empty. He glanced at Nora. She smiled in his direction.

The hands on the wall clock moved faster than Paul would have liked. One-twenty-five. The gallery settled down again. Paul turned to study the interested observers, then focused his attention on the courtroom door. *Come on April. Come through that door.*

But the courtroom doors remained motionless, and the din in the room quieted to a few whispers.

"Please rise." Paul's stomach dropped. Donna gave his hand a reassuring pat as they stood in unison. One more glance over his shoulder told Paul April Somersby had not made the judge's deadline. He gritted his teeth and glanced at the jury. Two members glared back at him. He gripped the table.

The judge walked slowly to her bench, glancing at the clock and the back of the courtroom. Then standing in front of her bench, surveying the courtroom, before taking her seat.

Donna leaned over and whispered in Paul's ear. "She'll be here."

But she wasn't here and time was up. Paul stared straight ahead and concentrated on keeping the anger out of his appearance.

"Ms. Hall. Have you heard from your colleague?"

Donna stood, taking her time to respond. A tactic that did not go unnoticed by the judge. "I asked you a question, Ms. Hall."

"Sorry your Honour. No, I have not heard from Ms. Somersby. But she'll be here. She's on her way. If you could just give her a couple more minutes, please."

The prosecutor jumped to his feet. "Your Honour. Respectfully, I think you've given Ms. Somersby enough extensions. I propose we proceed with closing statements."

The judge glanced to the back of the room before turning her attention on Donna. "Ms. Hall. Do you have the closing statements for Mr. Giovanni?"

Donna cleared her throat. "I do your Honour. But please, she's on her way. Just a few more minutes."

The courtroom bathed in silence. Not a whisper or even a creak of a bench, and most notable of all, not the sound of a door opening at the back of the courtroom.

Time stood still. Paul lowered his head and closed his eyes. April Somersby had passion, but she messed this up. They had the jury without having to prove the hair in her mailbox matched the hair found at the scene. What did that prove anyway? It wouldn't identify anyone else by name. This was a rookie mistake. Even he could see that. She should have known better.

Alienating the judge and jury did nothing for his case.

Paul thought back to the day he left Lori Trembley's house. The day she stitched him up and sent him on his way. The last time he saw her face. Their argument. His panic to leave her apartment. He'd seen a fancy sports car parked in the apartment parking lot as he ran by, but he hadn't looked any closer.

And why was John Smith helping him now? Maybe it was just his way of paying him back for the donation. The courtroom stood still as the prosecutor waited for the judge's response. The judge appeared to be weighing the options.

Donna dug into her briefcase and pulled out a folder labelled 'closing statement' in April's handwriting, and flipped it open. Bile rose in the back of Paul's throat.

He stared at the judge, her motions slow as Paul's mind savoured the before; the time where hope buoys the future as some place you want to go. But like a slow drowning, the tide's waves pounded that hope into submission, sucking the oxygen out of the room, and sliding over hope like it was never even there.

Paul reached for the glass of water in front of him to relieve the dizziness and ringing in his ears. When he glanced up, the judge stared straight at him. He shifted uncomfortably in his chair, but straightened and met the judge's gaze.

"I think we've wasted enough time waiting for Ms. Somersby."

Paul clasped his hands in his lap. This was it. His fate rested in the hands of a junior lawyer reading closing statements written by April. He couldn't have imagined a much worse ending.

The door opened, and Paul felt the breeze as the courtroom inhaled. Then April's heels punctuated the air with their familiar staccato rhythm. He wheeled around to watch her march down the centre aisle, like she'd planned her entrance exactly as it played out.

He turned toward the front of the courtroom and stared at the judge. Annoyance clouded her face, but something resembling relief held fast in her eyes. Donna rose and moved to the gallery, squeezing in to a back pew. April set her briefcase on the table in front of her and unzipped it, pulled out a red folder, and placed it on the table in front of her before she sat down.

"Ms. Somersby. You're late."

April rose to her feet. "Your Honour, my sincere apologies to you, the prosecution and this courtroom. Forty-eight hours is a tight timeframe to get the evidence I needed, and it turns out I needed a few more minutes than that. Please tell me I'm not too late to present my latest evidence?"

Paul inhaled. So, she got a match. If she had evidence, she had a match. The waters suffocating him receded and the ringing in his ears subsided. A strange calm took over him as he beamed up at April Somersby. *I should never have doubted you.*

"You came this close to being late." The judge gestured with her thumb and index finger millimetres apart. "Please proceed."

The prosecutor sat down, shaking his head in disgust.

"Your Honour, may I present DNA test results of the hair found in a Ziploc bag in my mailbox that is a perfect match for the hair found in Lori Trembley's hand at the scene of the crime? In addition, I'd like to provide the documents indicating the DNA from these hairs is not a match for the hair of my client."

April approached the bench, handing over the paperwork verifying her statements. Upon returning to her table, April grinned. "I'd like to call the molecular biologist who performed the testing, Dr. Strutt, to the witness stand."

A tall, slender, impeccably dressed woman strode down the aisle toward the front of the courtroom. After settling into the witness stand, Dr. Strutt turned her attention to April Somersby.

"Dr. Strutt, how long have you been a forensic molecular biologist?"

"I've been practicing molecular diagnostics for twenty years. The last ten of those years focusing on forensic genetics."

"Can you confirm for me you were the one who tested the sample of hair found in my mailbox?"

"Yes, I did."

"And did it have an initial signature of 'JS' on the front of the bag?"

"Yes."

"What did you find when you tested the hair?"

"I found the DNA map you presented to the judge. When

overlaid with the mapping of the DNA result from the hair at the scene of Lori Trembley's murder, they are an identical match."

"What about the blood at the scene? Does it also match the hair?"

"No, it does not."

"In your expert opinion, what does that mean?"

"It's simple. It means there were two people present with different DNA profiles at the scene."

"Could it also mean that perhaps one person was a chimera?" April turned toward the jury before elaborating. "Someone who has two sets of DNA?"

Dr. Strutt cocked her head to one side, considering the question. "Yes, it could mean that."

"And when is someone a chimera?"

"It happens more than people realize. When a pregnancy early on results in one embryo absorbing a twin embryo, you can get a chimera. A person who has two sets of DNA in different tissues. Someone with two different coloured eyes, for instance, is the most obvious sign of a chimera. But usually, people who are chimeras never become aware of it."

"What about bone marrow recipients? This court has already heard from another expert testifying bone marrow recipients have taken on their donor's DNA. Would you corroborate that testimony?"

"Yes, that's right. There's not a lot known about it yet, but it has been scientifically proven in bone marrow recipients and even other transplant recipients."

"So, in your expert opinion, could the person who Paul Giovanni donated bone marrow to back in 1982 have Paul's DNA in his blood and his own DNA in his hair?"

"Yes, that could be the case."

"And in your opinion, would you say it's more or less likely that the perpetrator of this crime was the recipient of Paul Giovanni's bone marrow donation, than Paul Giovanni?"

"More likely."

"And why would you say that?"

"The fact the hair and blood DNA don't match would point to the recipient of the bone marrow donation rather than the donor."

"Thank you Dr. Strutt. No further questions."

"Does the prosecution have questions for Dr. Strutt?"

The prosecutor rose and approached the witness stand. "Dr. Strutt, who gave you the Ziploc of hair?"

April grinned at the prosecutor. She'd expected this question.

"It was a police officer."

The prosecutor whirled in April's direction and took a deep breath before proceeding. "Was there a proper chain of custody of the sample?"

"Yes, the bag was sealed and a piece of tape with initials was unbroken when I received it. I never let it out of my sight and performed the testing myself."

"Thank you, Dr. Strutt. Just one more question. Would it be possible for there to be two perpetrators at the scene? One that matched the hair DNA and one that matched the blood DNA?

Dr. Strutt glanced at April before answering. "Yes, that could also be possible."

"No more questions, your Honour." The prosecutor turned toward his table, catching Paul's eye for a brief second before Paul turned away.

CHAPTER FORTY-FOUR
May 28, 2018

The weekend crawled by. Monday morning April arrived at the courthouse early and sat at the defence table in quiet reflection. She had done all she could. Facing DNA evidence was a tough uphill battle, but she felt confident she'd won. The quiet of the courtroom before others arrived calmed her nerves. She'd woken early, and had her cup of coffee without turning on the TV. She didn't need to hear the speculation touted as journalism on the news. The thought of breakfast made her stomach turn. The last few days nausea plagued her mornings.

Today she'd taken extra time to pick out the right outfit, a periwinkle blue pantsuit and a white silk blouse. The pants fit snugger than she remembered, and she eyed her figure in the mirror. Surely, she was too old to worry about nausea and a snug pant-suit? She shook off the thought and pulled her hair into a bun, before applying light make-up with extra concealer under her eyes to hide the black circles.

David Windsor hadn't responded to texts or reached out to her since he left her house four days ago. It wasn't like him, but her memory of the darkness she'd glimpsed in his eyes plagued her. Was he just too busy at work? Subconsciously, she stroked her abdomen before shaking her head and pulling out her closing statement from her briefcase, quickly skimming over it. People took their seats in the gallery behind her.

Paul entered from a side door, escorted by a bailiff. April rose to her feet and smiled. He looked good; shaven and wearing the outfit he'd worn his first day in court. She knew that wasn't an accident. He scanned the gallery and smiled, nodding his head toward where Nora and Zoe sat behind them. April pulled out his chair, and he sat down. She patted his shoulder.

"How are you holding up?"

Paul shook his head. "All things considered, pretty well, I guess. Just want it over with."

"It'll be over soon. Closing statements will be quick. The judge will review the jurors' duties and go over their responsibilities. She'll discuss reasonable doubt, and that's where we'll shine. There's no way they can ignore the doubt we've created." April patted Paul's shoulder. "It's going to go our way."

"I sure hope so. I know you've done all you can, and I'm grateful. No matter how this turns out, you've really gone above and beyond."

Paul stared at her with more sincerity than she'd ever seen in a defendant's eyes.

April didn't respond, just patted his shoulder once more.

"Please rise." Judge Alisha Munroe entered the courtroom, standing behind her bench, surveying the crowded gallery before settling into her chair.

April glanced at the prosecution. They appeared confident, more confident than they likely were.

The prosecution presented closing statements first. They made it sound like this was an open-and-closed case. DNA evidence, Paul at the scene the day of the murder, and perhaps accompanied by John Smith. It was a compelling argument.

April rose and strode over to the jurors. Pausing in front of them before speaking.

"The prosecution has presented their closing statement. They've told you how DNA matching Paul Giovanni was found at the scene of the crime. And how Paul Giovanni knew Lori Trembley and was at her apartment the day of her murder. But what the prosecution failed to remind you of, is the hair found in the fist of Lori Trembley. Hair that matched the DNA of hair found in a Ziploc bag signed with the initials 'JS' and left in my mailbox just a few days ago. That hair is crucial to this case. Why someone left that hair in my mailbox is a mystery. Perhaps John Smith, the recipient of Paul Giovanni's bone marrow donation, feels he owes Paul for that donation. But regardless of the reason, the evidence can't be overlooked. We've heard from expert witnesses that have explained how a bone marrow recipient could carry donor DNA in multiple tissues while retaining their own DNA in others, such as hair. That creates the reasonable doubt Judge Munroe will instruct you on today. The fact Paul Giovanni donated bone marrow to John Smith, a man who can't be located, a man who appears to have deliberately disappeared, creates that reasonable doubt. There's no gun or fingerprints pointing to Paul Giovanni. The only thing the prosecution has is DNA that could have been contributed by Paul Giovanni's bone marrow recipient."

April turned and strode toward Paul before whirling back to face the jury. "Paul Giovanni's past is flawed, but killing someone is not part of that past. We've presented evidence that creates doubt, reasonable doubt in this case. As Judge Munroe will outline, if you have reasonable doubt, you are duty bound to acquit Paul Giovanni in the murder of Lori Trembley."

April paused. "Thank you for your time and for accommodating the delays created by new evidence. Paul Giovanni, and I appreciate your participation in this trial."

April strode back to the defence table and took her seat. Paul sat motionless, as she'd instructed him. There was nothing left to do but wait. She'd done her job.

*****

Paul paced inside his cell. It had been six hours since the jury left for deliberations. He'd studied each face as April delivered her closing remarks. Two jurors nodded in agreement when she talked about reasonable doubt. But the rest remained expressionless, making it very difficult to tell which way they'd vote. During the prosecutor's closing statements three jurors smiled. What did that mean?

"Time to go."

Paul whirled around to face the door. "Go where?"

"Deliberations are over. Jury has come to a verdict. We're going back to the courtroom."

Paul's stomach turned. This was it. He closed his eyes and said a short prayer before being led out of his cell and into the van that would escort him to the courthouse.

April, Nora, and Zoe were seated in the courtroom when he entered. They smiled, and he nodded, but couldn't muster up the strength to smile back.

He sat down beside April. "So, what do you think this means? Six hours of deliberations?"

"I really don't know. I thought they'd be back within an hour." April patted the back of his hand resting on the table.

"So, it's not a good sign, then?" Paul swallowed the lump rising in the back of his throat.

"Really, there's no way to tell. Let's not jump to conclusions." April smiled faintly.

"All rise."

Judge Munroe entered the courtroom. She droned on, but at last the words Paul had been waiting for cut through the air. "What say the jury?"

A tall, slender woman rose and made her way to the microphone. Paul stared at the clock. Seconds ticked in slow motion. How many seconds had passed since his arrest? How many more would be wasted? He turned to glance at Nora. Tears brimmed her eyes, and she mouthed, *I love you.* He cleared his throat and turned back to the jury.

"Your Honour, we find the defendant not guilty..."

Paul stopped listening. Had he heard right? He watched April rise to her feet, and he did the same. She grabbed him with both arms and pulled him in for a hug. His knees buckled, but she held him up.

Judge Munroe's gavel hit the bench. She said words, but the only ones Paul heard were, "Court dismissed."

In an instant, Nora and Zoe were hugging him. The jury set him free.

CHAPTER FORTY-FIVE
June 11, 2018

Paul wandered from room to room, restless. He'd spent enough time in segregation to find being alone, uncomfortable. He wandered into the living room and eyed the bookshelf on the wall beside the fireplace. The paperback he'd started all those months ago beckoned him. He pulled it down and settled on the couch to read, but his mind wandered to the time before. Finally, he gave in and laid the book on his chest, closing his eyes. Maybe it was a nap he needed.

The doorbell rang, interrupting his solitude and instantly increasing his heart rate. In one deft move, he placed the paperback on the coffee table and rose to his feet. That doorbell would forever more cause him anxiety. He glanced out the window. A red sports car sat in the driveway. At first, he wondered what April Somersby could want, but then realized it was an Aston Martin, not a Lexus. The hall stretched out in front of him as he walked to the door; the handle cold in his hand and he took a deep breath before turning it. Familiar eyes stared into his and caused his knees to buckle. He held on to the door for support.

John opened the screen door separating them. Paul regained his composure and backed down the hallway. His fear turning to rage. "What the hell's the matter with you? What're you doing here, John?"

John Smith stepped through the doorway and let the screen door close behind him. The latch punctuating the silence. He grinned and winked at Paul. "Nice to see you too, buddy."

"You're not my buddy. Do you know the risk you're taking? Why're you here?" Paul glanced at his watch. "Nora and Zoe could be back any minute."

"We both know that's not true." John glanced at his watch. "They're at the spa, and by my calculations, just getting settled in on their respective massage tables."

Paul swallowed.

"I just wanted to touch base. It's been a long time since we've talked." John's grin caught Paul off guard. It wasn't malicious or gloating. It was a grin that drew him in.

"So, talk. I've got nothing to say." Paul folded his arms in front of him.

"Now, don't be like that. We're a good team. I kept you out of a guilty verdict, didn't I?"

"Oh, I'm supposed to thank you for not letting me go down for a crime you committed?" Paul clenched his teeth, working his jaw back and forth. "But tell me, why did you help me?"

"I thought I'd pay back your kindness. I mean, you saved my life with that bone marrow donation back in the day."

"Oh, come on. There's got to be more to it than that." Paul stepped back, trying to put more distance between them as if it would somehow erase their connection.

John cleared his throat and used his foot to remove a wrinkle from the mat he stood on. "Truth be told, I couldn't let you take credit for my hit. The gang that gave me the hit on Lori Trembley didn't like the thought I took credit for a job I didn't do. I needed to set the record straight if I'm to keep working in the industry. I'm not ready to retire yet."

"I knew you weren't getting me off out of the goodness of your heart." Paul glared at John. "So, why're you here?"

"I don't like loose ends. And you've just become one. You're the only person who could identify me as the infamous John Smith."

Paul raised his hands in defence and took another step back.

"Relax, I won't hurt you. No need when I have insurance in my back pocket."

"Yeah, what kind of insurance would that be?" Paul peered past John as he noted a car drive by.

John remained rooted to the spot. "We both know what really happened at Lori Trembley's that day. I'm sure you don't want anyone finding out the whole truth now, do you? Especially her brothers or members of the Riley Park gang or Big Circle Boys."

Paul stared at John, opened his mouth, then closed it again before speaking. "When I left Lori Trembley, she was alive." The crack in Paul's voice betrayed any bluster he tried to marshal.

"What makes you so sure? When I found her, she laid in a pool of her own blood. A shattered glass coffee table surrounding her. When I leaned over to check for a pulse, she grabbed my hair and brought me to my knees on a pile of glass. When she released her grip on me, I fell backwards before stumbling to my feet. Blood soaked the carpet and ran down my legs, distracting me for a moment. She managed to stand before I got a shot off. It was a sloppy job, I'll admit."

Paul shook his head. "How could you? Why'd you have to kill her? I never meant for her to get hurt. We argued. She stepped back and fell onto the coffee table. I never laid a hand on her. I panicked and ran, stopping at a payphone down the block to call the cops and tell them I heard fighting and glass breaking at Lori's apartment."

John's eyes softened. "She was the first job I ever did. Out of all the jobs I've had over the years, hers still haunts me." John paused before raising his eyes to meet Paul's. "I saw you leave her apartment that day. I was at the end of the hall when you caught the elevator down. Of course, you were too far away for me to recognize, but when the news reported they charged you with her murder, I realized who I'd seen that day. You haven't changed a bit. I couldn't get over the coincidence that we were both there at the same time. I swear I didn't know you knew her."

Paul's voice dropped. "Would it have made any difference if you had? If you knew I was a friend of hers, would that have stopped you from killing her?"

There was a long pause before John responded. "No, it was my first job. I needed to follow through. I realize now you didn't want to hurt her, but all our actions have consequences, even ones we think are kind gestures. Like bone marrow donations." John grinned and stepped closer.

Paul grabbed an umbrella in the stand next to the closet.

John raised his hands and stepped back. "Hey, I just wanted to have a chat."

Paul's eyes widened. "And I want nothing to do with you. Leave."

"Okay, okay. But before I go, I have to ensure you understand something. They might find your DNA at a few crime scenes. And unless I'm careful, your life might be under scrutiny for as long as I continue to work. You see, I don't have any worry about hair incriminating me anymore." John took off his hat and revealed a newly shorn head, the same bald head Paul faced in 1982 at their meeting after the donation.

Paul stepped forward and opened the screen door. He grabbed the collar of John's coat and dragged him out onto the step. His heart raced; blood pounded in his ears. He glanced down the street. Thankfully, this time Mrs. Campbell was nowhere to be seen.

John took a deep breath and lowered his voice to a whisper. "I hate to remind you of this, but I need to protect myself. Remember, I know where you live. I know where your wife works and where your daughter goes to school. And the brothers of Lori Trembley? Can you imagine what they'd do if they knew how you left her?" John cocked his head to one side and stared intently into Paul's eyes. "So, remember, this visit never happened. And you'd never be able to identify me in a police lineup, right?"

Paul managed to nod.

John strode toward his car and opened the door before turning back to Paul. "I hate to have to return this rental, but it's my only regret when it comes to leaving this town." He climbed in and the engine roared to life. John raised his hand as if waving goodbye to a good friend, but his unblinking stare sent a shiver down Paul's spine.

ABOUT THE AUTHOR

Heather Dawn Gray is a creative writer with a long career in laboratory medicine. After 25 years in healthcare, she obtained her Master of Arts in Communications and Technology, formalizing forty years of dabbling in fiction and non-fiction.

Canada is proudly the country Heather calls home, but Australia also holds a place in her heart. She has visited several other countries, drawing inspiration from people and places along the way.

It was her own DNA test in 2018 that revealed surprises leading her to question 'What if…' resulting in the birth of her first fiction novel, 'The Lie' and its sequel 'Where Truth Lies'.

'Consequences' follows in the wake of that duology because, well, there are so many 'what ifs' to pursue when it comes to DNA testing.

Heather currently resides in Edmonton, Alberta Canada with her soulmate, Ron. They have two daughters, Sabra and Colby, who are pursuing their professional careers in Canada and Australia.

Website: https://www.graystar.tech/published-novels.html

Made in United States
North Haven, CT
19 July 2023

39290231R00153